# AMITI

# Cold Games Part II

*The Game of Secrets*

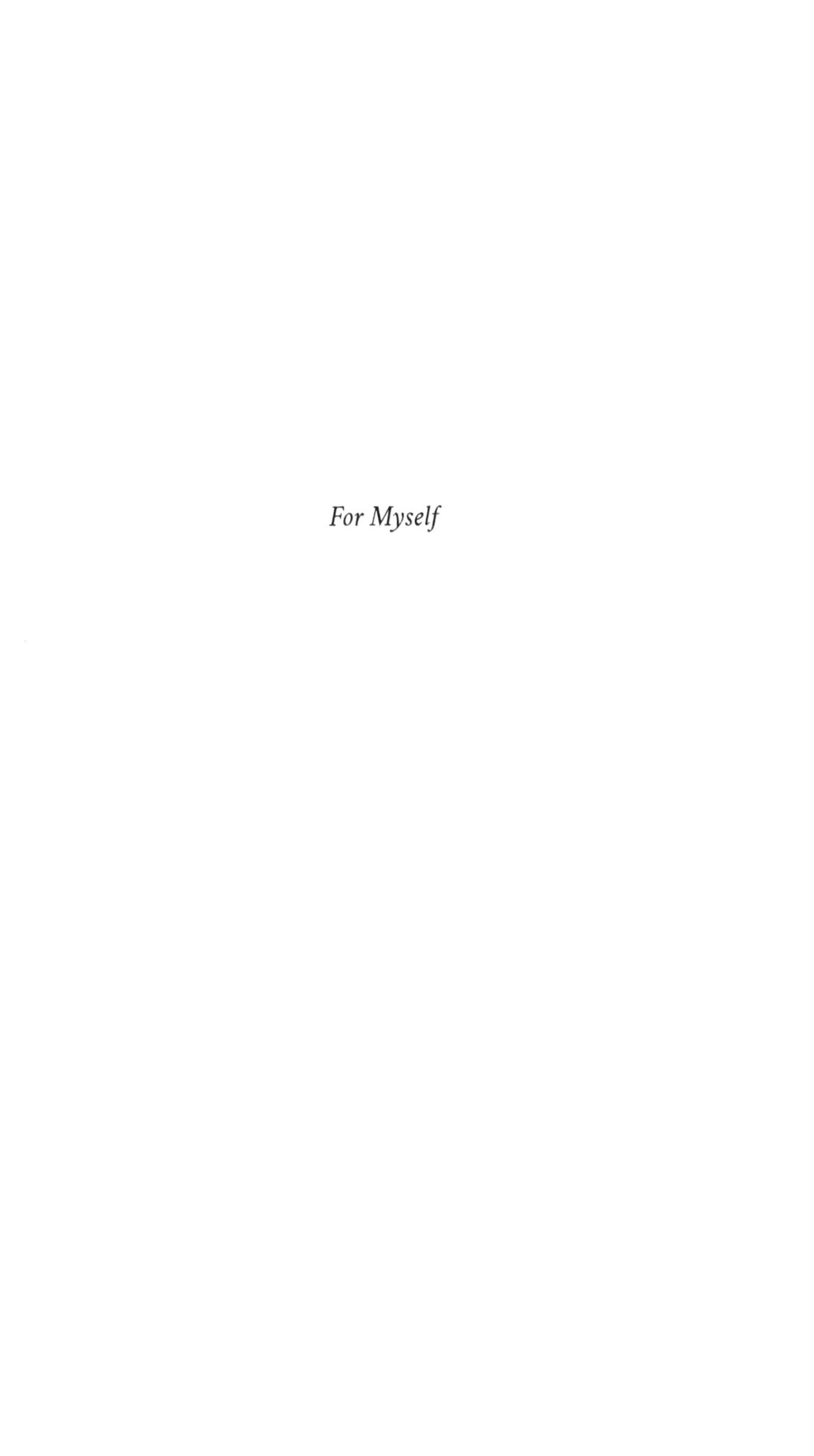

*For Myself*

Reality is always soft clay,
ever shifting and changing its shape.
Fire it into form, and
at the very moment
you are hailing it as final truth
it will break in your hands.


~Dorothy Walters
NO MATTER WHAT YOU KNOW
(AN EXTRACT)

# Contents

*Cold Games Part 2: The Game of Secrets* is the sequel to *Cold Games: A Game of Confusion*. For the best experience and full understanding of the characters, their journeys, and the events that have led to this story, it is recommended to read the first book before diving into this one.

# Recap of the Prequel; Cold Games Part I: The Game of Confusion

Asterine Ashworth, a bold and rebellious teenager, gets sent to Harlow Academy, a boarding school hidden in a forest in Texas, after pulling one prank too many. But Harlow isn't an ordinary school—it's full of supernatural secrets. Asterine's life changes dramatically as she discovers a world filled with danger, mystery, and magic.

At Harlow, Asterine reunites with her old friends Maeve, Jocosa, and Fabian, who vanished from her life without explanation. She finds out that Evander, her manipulative and dangerous ex-boyfriend, forced them to leave. Evander, who is a siren with the power to control minds, holds a deep grudge against Asterine for breaking up with him and rejecting his dark side.

As Asterine digs deeper into the school's mysteries, she meets Ryker Reed, Evander's older half-brother. Ryker's past is filled with pain, including being cursed and trapped in a magical prison called the Silver Circle. Though they start off clashing, Asterine and Ryker grow closer and work together to stop Evander's schemes.

The turning point comes when Asterine discovers she is a siphoner, someone who can absorb magic from others and use it herself. She uses this newfound power to defeat Evander

"

and free her friends from his control. With help from Ryker, Jocosa's spells, and Fabian's bravery, they overcome Evander. However, instead of destroying him, they let him live, and he remains at Harlow, keeping everyone on edge.

The story is about betrayal, forgiveness, and self-discovery as Asterine begins to understand her powers, strengthen her friendships, and uncover long-hidden family secrets.

# Prologue

Underestimation is a curse. People don't realize that when they choose not to tell you something important, they're setting you up to stumble through the dark. How can anyone expect you to act, to handle things, when they've kept you in the shadows? It's frustrating to be judged as incapable and, worse, to be denied the knowledge that could help you prove otherwise.

When a situation involves you, it's only natural to be let in on it. But people seem to take it upon themselves to decide what you should know. They assume they're protecting you—or maybe they just don't trust you enough to handle the truth. Either way, they don't stop to consider how you'll feel when you eventually find out they kept it from you.

And here's the kicker: if you don't know what's happening, how are you supposed to prove your strength? How are you supposed to show them they were wrong to doubt you?

In my life, I'm used to nature throwing challenges at me that force me to uncover the truth on my own. No matter how well people think they can hide things, the truth has a way of finding you. It's inevitable; it's your truth, after all. And in the end, no one—not even the most powerful paranormal—can defy the natural order.

Maybe, if you didn't have to face the truth meant for you, you could live peacefully, free from its burdens. But fate doesn't let go so easily. Sometimes, the truth takes its time coming to you. And other times, it hits like a tsunami, all at once and too much to handle. Destiny, fate, coincidence—they're all just pieces of nature's design.

Eventually, the truth reaches you. And when it does, you're the only one who can make sense of it. For me, though, it's not enough just to understand. I'm driven to prove everyone wrong, to show them they underestimated the wrong person.

*Especially my mother.*

# 1

# Frustration

"Asterine?" Eira's voice pulls me back to reality. She's standing across the room, disheveled but resilient, like she just returned from hell. Her hollow eyes meet mine, and her brunette hair is a tangled mess. I can tell her spirit's still there, even after everything she's been through. Normally, I'd run over to hug her, relieved to see her standing in one piece, but right now, I'm locked in my own shock, reeling from this new revelation.

I open my mouth, ready to share what's racing through my mind, when an abrupt, thunderous knock on the door jolts me. I jump, my heart racing. Fabian, my former best friend-turned-reluctant traitor, steps toward the door, rolling his eyes. "Whoever that is, they sure know how to pick their timing," he mutters, his voice laced with sarcasm.

I clench my fists, a wave of fear rising within me. What if it's Evander outside, somehow back and angrier than ever? Neville seems to sense my dread; he moves closer, squeezing my hand in silent support. His presence is grounding, a reminder of the quiet, wordless connection we've always shared. My twin brother—who's somehow alive again—is here with me, like we're stepping back into a rhythm we lost long ago.

Behind Fabian, Ryker positions himself defensively. He's the boy I met at Harlow, with a connection to my ex, Evander—a connection that remains complicated and unsettling. Jocosa stands nearby, her face a mask of tension, her blonde hair fraying at the edges. She looks as frightened as the stray cat Ryker accidentally startled in the academy garden the night I arrived.

"You're sure you want to open that?" Jocosa asks in a hushed tone, her voice barely above a whisper.

Fabian scoffs, his hand on the doorknob. "Got another option?" He shoots her a grim look, then swings the door open.

And there, of all people, stands…Headmaster Dimick. My mind races with confusion. What's he doing here, now? His sharp gaze sweeps the room, and something about his expression tells me we're in trouble—deep, no-getting-out-of-it trouble. It takes every ounce of restraint not to roll my eyes. Figures that he'd finally catch up with us after our spotty attendance over the past week.

"Headmaster Dimick?" Maeve echoes my thoughts, her voice soft but full of tension. She, Fabian, and Jocosa—my friend group from back in California—had been compelled to come to Harlow by Evander, the siren who once claimed to care for me. All the while, I'd thought they'd vanished from my life without a trace.

"Hello to you too, Maeve," Mr. Dimick replies dryly, stepping into the room and making it feel uncomfortably cramped. I can practically feel the walls closing in around us, the atmosphere thick with anticipation. I swear, if anyone else decides to show up, I'll start hyperventilating.

Ryker steps forward. "I assume we're in trouble?" he asks, breaking the silence. It's like everyone in the room has a direct line to my thoughts.

"Oh, you most definitely are," Mr. Dimick replies, his tone steely. He scans each of us in turn, then commands, "Everyone, to my office. Now. And you too, Mr. Ashworth," he adds, directing a look at Neville. My heart skips a beat. How does he know my brother?

As we follow him down the long, Gothic hallways of Harlow Academy, the air is thick with tension. The walls are lined with elaborate, haunting tapestries, scenes woven into the fabric in dark, muted colors. They're eerie yet captivating, as though the images hide secrets of their own. I can't shake the feeling that I've seen them before, even though I can't quite place where.

When we reach his office, we file in and stand in a tense line, waiting for whatever judgment he's about to pass down. Mr. Dimick settles into the large leather chair behind his desk, looking at us with that unnervingly calm gaze.

"Do you know why you're all here?" he asks, his voice steady.

"Yeah, we haven't exactly been attending our classes," I start, but he cuts me off with a dismissive wave of his hand.

"That's not the real reason," he says coolly. "Do you have any idea just how much danger you were all in, going to The Silver Circle?" He barely pauses for us to react before continuing, "And you, Miss Ashworth—blowing up Evander Reed? What were you even thinking?"

Shock roots me to the spot, and I struggle to respond. Before I can say anything, Eira blurts out, "How do you know?" It's like she plucked the thought straight from my mind. I can't help but wonder if everyone's able to read my thoughts, or if we're all just trapped in the same confusion.

Mr. Dimick's piercing gaze lands on her. "I know everything that happens in my school," he replies smoothly.

"What are you?" I blurt out, my voice sounding braver than I feel.

His expression darkens as he studies me, then he glances at Neville with a thoughtful look. Without a word, he begins pacing around the office, giving me a chance to take in the place. It's large, surprisingly so, with wooden furniture polished to a high shine. His desk, the chairs, the cabinets—everything is carved from different types of wood, from rich mahogany to gleaming maple. Each piece looks carefully chosen, fitting the Gothic aura of the academy.

"A warlock," he finally says, stopping to face us.

"With an impeccable sense of trouble," Ryker mutters beside me. His unexpected sarcasm almost makes me laugh, but I stifle it as Mr. Dimick's lips twitch in a smirk.

"Yes, a paranormal," he continues, and there's a strange satisfaction in his voice.

I stare at him, trying to process what this means, when he turns to Neville. "It's time, Neville. Tell her everything—and then go meet your family."

Neville starts to argue, "But we shouldn't involve her, it's—" He's cut off as Ryker leans in, whispering something to him. I can't see Ryker's face from where I'm standing, but the intensity between him and Mr. Dimick suggests they're exchanging more than words.

"Very well," Mr. Dimick finally says, leaning back in his chair. "In any case, I expect to see at least two A's on your weekly tests. All of you." His tone makes it clear that this is not a suggestion.

Eira pipes up suddenly. "What about homecoming?" Her voice carries a mix of hope and disappointment.

Mr. Dimick's brows furrow. "Homecoming was three days ago."

"Three days?" I echo, startled.

"Yes," he says, as if it's common knowledge.

"But we thought it was tomorrow," Eira stammers, her face paling.

"What's today?" I manage to ask, trying to wrap my mind around what he's saying.

"September 17th," Mr. Dimick replies nonchalantly.

Shock tightens my chest as I glance around. Only Eira and I look surprised; everyone else stares at the floor, clearly hiding something. My mind races, trying to make sense of how we lost three days without anyone telling us.

"Alright, that's enough," Mr. Dimick says briskly, dismissing us as if our whole world hasn't just been upturned. "Off you go. Best of luck on your tests."

As we file out of his office, questions burn inside me. What's happening? And why is everyone around me keeping secrets?

2

# Homesick

Maeve, Jocosa, and Fabian head straight to their dorm from Headmaster Dimick's office, each of them looking drained. After everything we've been through, who wouldn't be exhausted? Yet, for some reason, I feel wired—like I'm riding the high of ten cups of coffee. Adrenaline courses through me, my mind whirling too fast to settle.

Back in my dorm room, it's just me, Eira, Neville, and Ryker. We stand in an awkward circle, eyes downcast, none of us daring to break the silence. There's so much to talk about—so many answers I'm desperate for—but now isn't the right time. Besides, I know that if I push too hard, Neville might just clam up. And as if I needed more pressure, Headmaster Dimick's little demand for "at least two A's" on the upcoming tests hangs over us like a storm cloud.

Eira clears her throat, shuffling toward her nightstand to pick up her phone. She looks back at us, her expression unreadable. "Um, I think I'll crash with Eve tonight. Text me if you need anything," she says.

"You sure?" I ask, starting to offer a place for her to stay, but she cuts me off with a small smile.

"It's fine, Asterine. You have a lot to catch up on with your brother, and I could really use a full night's sleep," she says, shrugging as if that explains everything. When she puts it that way, what can I say? I manage a nod.

"Thank you," Neville says, but his expression tells another story. I know he's hoping I'll drop the questions tonight and let him off the hook. Well, he's got another thing coming.

Eira slips out the door, leaving just the three of us. Ryker looks just as tired as she did, his eyes heavy as he glances between Neville and me. "I'll see you guys tomorrow," he mutters, moving to leave as well. Neville lets out a loud sigh, clearly relieved.

"Wait," I call out. Ryker pauses, turning back to look at me. Taking a deep breath, I step closer. "Thank you, Ryker. For everything," I say, my voice softer than I intended.

He nods, a faint smile on his lips. "Night, Asterine," he says, his voice warm, before turning to leave.

"Night, Ryker," I reply, watching him disappear down the hall.

The door clicks shut, and Neville groans. "Oh god, I think I'm going to die again."

I turn to face him, arching an eyebrow. "Not until you answer my questions, twin," I say, crossing my arms.

He groans again, half-laughing. "Now? Really, Asterine?"

"Yeah, really," I reply firmly. "People have been hiding things from me for the past two years, Neville. I deserve the truth."

He raises his hands in surrender. "Can I at least take a shower first?"

I roll my eyes but nod. "Fine." As he heads for the bathroom,

I rummage through my wardrobe, pulling out a baggy T-shirt and shorts that should fit him well enough. After two years, he looks exactly the same, like he stepped out of some warped time loop, and my clothes should fit him just fine.

As I sit on the bed, I notice my phone buzzing. The screen lights up with *Mom calling*. Of all the times for her to reach out. I've been dodging her calls for weeks now, but if I keep it up, she might just show up and lecture me in person. With a sigh, I answer.

"Hello?" I say, trying to keep my tone neutral.

"Asterine! Finally, you pick up! I've been so worried. What's been going on?" My mom's voice is a mix of relief and concern.

"Relax, Mom. I'm fine," I say, forcing a casual tone. "Just busy with school." A partial truth is better than nothing.

"Oh," she sighs, sounding oddly disappointed. "How have you been?"

"I'm okay. How are you and Dad?" I ask, feeling the familiar tension creeping in.

"We're both great! Missing you, of course," she replies, and her words feel like a punch. *They miss me now?* She didn't seem so sentimental when she practically pushed me out the door to come here.

She pauses, and then I hear my dad's voice in the background. "Hey, Asterine!" he calls out, his voice slightly muffled. "Your mom's been keeping me updated. We miss you, Asterine."

"Miss you too, Dad. I'll be visiting after my tests," I say, more for their sake than mine.

"Oh…well, that's wonderful to hear," he says, though there's an odd hesitation in his voice. "Alright, see you soon!"

We exchange quick goodbyes, and I hang up, plugging in my phone to charge. The conversation leaves a strange taste in my mouth. They sent me here without a second thought, and now they're acting like they're the ones who've been abandoned. I can't help but feel like a burden to them—an inconvenience they're relieved to be rid of.

Another day full of surprises. Is this what it means to be kept in the dark about my own life? I lean back, my mind a tangle of resentment and unanswered questions. People think they're protecting me by hiding the truth, but all they're doing is making me question everything. Every person has a purpose, a role they're meant to play, and right now, I feel like I'm stumbling around, blindfolded, trying to figure out what that is. And whatever secrets my family is hiding…they're tied to that purpose.

I glance at the bathroom door, wondering how long Neville will take. After twenty minutes, he finally steps out, his hair damp, a towel wrapped around his waist.

"Asterine—" he begins, but I cut him off, pointing to the foot of the bed where I left the oversized clothes.

"Wear those," I say, not in the mood for more stalling.

"Thanks, lifesaver," he mutters, reaching for the clothes before heading back into the bathroom.

"You owe me," I call after him. "For saving your life *and* for the clothes!"

When he reappears, dressed in my baggy T-shirt and shorts that somehow suit him perfectly, I can't help but smirk. "Your style's improved," he quips, mocking me. But I don't rise to the bait. I fix him with a glare that says *cut the games*.

"What's wrong?" he asks, coming to sit across from me on the bed, though he looks like he'd rather be anywhere else.

"Mom called," I say, watching his reaction carefully.

He stiffens, and I catch a flicker of worry in his eyes. "You didn't tell her, did you?"

"No, I didn't," I reply, unable to hide the sarcasm. He breathes a sigh of relief, like he's been holding it in for ages.

"So…what did 'Mother dearest' say?" he asks, trying to lighten the mood, but I'm not about to let him change the subject.

I narrow my eyes at him, keeping my tone icy. "You don't get to ask questions, not until you answer mine."

Neville rolls his eyes, but he knows I'm not letting this go. "You haven't changed a bit," he teases, but I only stare him down, my patience wearing thin.

Seeing that I'm serious, he finally raises his hands in defeat. "Alright, alright. Ask away."

# 3

# Questions and Neville

"What happened in Dimick's office, Neville?" I ask, my arms crossed as I stare at him.

"Oh, you know, he's just a warlock messing with you," Neville says nonchalantly, leaning back against Eira's bed frame.

"If that's the case, then how the hell does he know you?" I press, not willing to let him sidestep this.

Neville rolls his eyes, as if the answer should be obvious. "Because I'm famous," he replies with a smug grin.

I glare at him. "You're impossible."

Instead of pushing him further, I switch tactics. "Fine. How did you survive? I thought…" My voice catches. "I thought you were dead."

He sighs, his expression softening just slightly. "Your petty boyfriend found out who Ryker really was, and I was helping Ryker erase his face from Evander's head. Let's just say Evander didn't take kindly to that."

"Firstly, he's my *ex-*," I snap.

"Oh, what a relief," Neville interrupts, throwing his hands

in the air theatrically. "Finally."

Ignoring his jab, I continue, "Secondly, why were you helping Ryker? And thirdly, we *saw* your body, Nev."

His face darkens. "Ryker's been my best friend since childhood, Asterine. If you weren't so caught up in your own little world, you'd have noticed." Before I can react to the sting of his words, he keeps going. "Anyway, Evander was stronger than we thought. He had backup. Things went sideways, and honestly, I don't remember much after I blacked out. So I don't know what you mean about seeing my dead body." He pauses for breath, then adds, "But at least Ryker and I succeeded. He erased himself from Evander's mind."

I gape at him, my thoughts spinning. "You erased him from Evander's memory? What does that even mean?" The words feel foreign on my tongue.

Neville just shrugs. "It's a thing paranormal beings can do. Let's leave it at that."

I open my mouth to argue but quickly shut it again, realizing I have no idea where to start. My thoughts are a swirling mess, leaving me staring at him like a wide-eyed goldfish.

"Any more questions?" Neville asks, raising an eyebrow. When I don't respond, still too stunned to speak, he takes that as a cue to end the conversation. He stands and moves toward Eira's bed, which he claims for the night.

"I figured," he mutters, climbing under the covers. "Goodnight, Sis. And don't stay up too late." He winks at me before turning over and falling asleep almost instantly.

But I can't sleep. There are too many unanswered questions, and my mind refuses to settle. Every answer Neville gives just creates more confusion. My frustration builds until suddenly, something happens.

My vision goes blank, and a sharp, pounding sensation seizes my head. My veins feel like they're on fire, and a strange, electric sensation courses through me. Panic sets in as I realize I can't move, like I'm trapped inside my own body. I clench my fists and bring them to my temples, desperate to hold onto some sense of control.

Then, like the snap of a thunderstorm, the tension breaks. The room stills, and I blink as my vision clears.

"What the—" Neville's voice comes from somewhere behind me.

I whirl around to find Eira's entire bed—frame, mattress, sheets, and all—crammed into the far corner of the room. Neville is sprawled on the floor underneath the heap, with pillows, books, and even Eira's nightstand lamp scattered around him.

"Oh my god!" I rush over, horrified. Neville glares up at me from beneath the mess, his face a mix of shock and irritation.

"What are you doing standing there? Help me!" he yells.

I cross my arms and smirk. "Admiring my artwork," I reply, but I quickly move to pull the debris off him. Once free, Neville scrambles to his feet, glaring at me as he puts as much distance as possible between us.

"I've been back for half a day, and you're already trying to kill me!" he exclaims.

I snort. "Oh, stop being dramatic. You're fine."

He points a finger at me accusingly. "Do you and your ex share the same motive or what?"

Ignoring his ranting, I start picking up the mess I caused.

"Wait," Neville says, his tone sharp. "What are you doing?"

I look up at him, puzzled. "Fixing this so you can sleep. Isn't it obvious?"

"With your hands?" he asks incredulously.

"What else would I use?" I mutter, already tired of this conversation.

Neville stares at me like I've just said something insane. "Asterine, you're a siphoner. You caused this mess with leftover power from The Silver Circle. You can use that same power to fix it."

My hands freeze mid-motion. "I... can?" I blink, completely thrown.

"Hasn't anyone ever told you this?" Neville looks genuinely exasperated.

His words hit me like a punch to the gut. "No one tells me *anything*, Neville," I say quietly, my voice trembling. "Everyone's hiding something from me, and I can feel it. Every single day."

The room falls silent, and for a moment, I let the weight of my words settle between us. I've been here a month, thrown into a world I barely understand. I know the paranormal exists. I know I'm part of it. But that's all I know. Everyone around me acts like I should have all the answers, but they keep leaving me in the dark. The hypocrisy of it all is maddening.

Neville doesn't say a word, just watches me with an unreadable expression. For a moment, I wonder why I even expected him to comfort me. He's been through hell himself, and I'm here bombarding him with questions like he owes me something.

A wave of guilt crashes over me. Maybe I shouldn't be so hard on him. Maybe I've been so wrapped up in my own confusion that I forgot he's been suffering too. I let out a shaky breath, feeling the beginnings of another anxiety spiral creeping in. I need a distraction—anything to keep me from falling apart again.

# 4

# Internal deviation

The silence in the room feels heavy, almost suffocating. Neville is still watching me with that maddening, unreadable expression, his arms crossed as he leans against Eira's disheveled nightstand. The mess I created remains scattered around the room—a stark reminder of my complete lack of control. My twin brother, the one person I should feel completely at ease with, is now both my accuser and my only guide.

"Fine," Neville finally says, his voice breaking the tension. "If you're going to survive as a siphoner, you need to learn how to control that… whatever that was." He gestures vaguely toward the heap of furniture in the corner. "And you're going to start now."

I blink at him, startled. "Now? As in *right now*?"

"Yes, Asterine. Now," he says firmly, pushing off the nightstand and striding toward me. His tone leaves no room for argument, but I can't stop the unease curling in my stomach. My hands are already clammy, my pulse quickening. "The longer you wait, the harder it gets to control leftover power.

It's like static—it builds up and goes haywire if you don't channel it."

I glance at the wreckage and back at Neville, swallowing hard. "What if I make it worse?"

Neville snorts, shaking his head. "Worse than launching a bed and almost flattening me? That's a pretty high bar, Sis." His teasing tone does little to calm me, but his eyes soften as he adds, "Look, you're not going to mess this up. I'll guide you."

The word *guide* rings in my ears. It feels so surreal to think of Neville as my mentor in anything. He's my twin—the boy who used to prank me, who knew every button to push to drive me insane. And now, he's the only person who can help me navigate this insane world of siphoners and powers I barely understand.

"Okay," I whisper, more to myself than to him. "Okay. Tell me what to do."

Neville steps closer, his voice dropping into a calm, steady rhythm. "First, stop overthinking."

"Not possible," I mutter under my breath, earning a smirk from him.

"Close your eyes," he instructs, ignoring my sarcasm. "Focus on your breathing."

I hesitate but do as he says. My eyelids flutter shut, and the world around me fades into darkness. My breaths come shallow at first, erratic. The mess in the room, my pounding heart, Neville's judgment—all of it swirls in my head like a tornado.

"Deeper," Neville says gently. "Breathe deeper. In through your nose, out through your mouth. Match my pace."

I listen to the steady rhythm of his breathing and mimic it, drawing in a slow breath and exhaling just as slowly. After a few repetitions, my heart begins to settle, and the swirling thoughts in my mind ease into a dull hum.

"Good," Neville says. "Now, reach inside yourself. Feel for the power."

"Feel for the power?" I echo skeptically, my voice barely above a whisper. "What does that even mean?"

"It's hard to explain," he admits, his voice tinged with patience. "It's like… a spark. A warmth. You'll know it when you find it."

I focus inward, searching for something—anything—that feels like the spark Neville described. At first, there's nothing. Just the steady thrum of my heartbeat and the cool, empty void in my mind. But then, faintly, I sense it: a flicker of warmth deep in my chest, like the tiniest ember of a fire.

"I think I feel it," I murmur.

"Good. Now, hold onto it. Don't let it go," Neville says. His voice sharpens slightly as he adds, "And whatever you do, don't force it. Power like this doesn't respond well to brute strength. It's about channeling, not commanding."

Easier said than done. The ember within me feels fragile, like a candle flame in a storm. I reach for it cautiously, wrapping my awareness around it as if cradling something precious. The warmth spreads slowly, radiating outwards in faint tendrils.

"It's growing," I say, my voice trembling with awe.

"Stay with it," Neville encourages. "Now, picture what you want it to do. Visualize the mess fixing itself—Eira's bed upright, the nightstand back in place, everything where it belongs."

I try to focus on his words, but the sensation of the power moving through me is so strange, so overwhelming, that my thoughts scatter like leaves in the wind. The warmth is no longer just an ember; it's a roaring flame now, surging through my veins with a life of its own. My skin prickles, and a low hum fills my ears, growing louder with each passing second.

"Don't lose it, Asterine!" Neville's voice cuts through the noise like a lifeline. "Stay in control."

I grit my teeth, forcing myself to focus. In my mind's eye, I see the room as it should be—Eira's bed neatly in place, the books stacked on the nightstand, the lamp upright. I cling to that image, willing the power to obey.

The heat within me grows hotter, almost unbearable, and then—like a dam breaking—it rushes outward. My eyes snap open just in time to see the room transform. The bed slides across the floor, straightening itself as if guided by invisible hands. The books leap back onto the nightstand, and the lamp stands upright once more. Even the charging cable coils neatly into place.

I stare, wide-eyed and breathless, as the last traces of chaos vanish. The room is whole again, as if nothing had ever happened.

"You did it," Neville says, his voice filled with a mix of pride and relief.

I can't speak. My hands tremble at my sides, still tingling from the aftershock of the power I unleashed. The heat in my chest has receded, leaving behind a strange emptiness—like a vacuum where the power once burned.

"That was…" I trail off, struggling to find the right words.

"Intense?" Neville supplies with a grin.

I nod, still too overwhelmed to form a coherent sentence. My mind races with questions. How did I do that? How did the power know where to go, what to fix? Was it me guiding it, or was it something else entirely?

"You're a natural," Neville says, clapping me on the shoulder. "Most siphoners can't channel power like that on their first try."

I blink at him, incredulous. "That was my first try?"

"Well, technically your second," he says with a smirk, gesturing toward the corner where the bed had been launched. "But let's not count that."

I manage a weak laugh, though my knees feel like they might give out at any moment. "Neville, what happens if I can't control it next time?"

"You will," he says confidently. "It's like riding a bike. The more you practice, the easier it gets."

His words are meant to reassure me, but they only add to the weight pressing on my shoulders. If this is what I'm capable of now, what will happen when I have even more power? The thought both thrills and terrifies me.

Neville must sense my unease because he steps in front of me, his expression softening. "You're not alone in this, Asterine. I'll help you figure it out. And Ryker will too. You've got people who've got your back."

I nod, swallowing the lump in my throat. For the first time in a long time, I feel a glimmer of hope. Maybe I can figure this out. Maybe I can learn to control the chaos within me.

But deep down, I know this is only the beginning.

# 5

# Midnight eyes

Neville is snoring softly, sprawled on Eira's bed with the blanket half-hanging off the edge. The quiet rise and fall of his chest is steady, a stark contrast to the chaos of my thoughts. I lie in my bed, staring at the ceiling, the faint glow of moonlight casting soft shadows on the walls. Sleep won't come—not tonight.

No matter how much I try to empty my mind, it always circles back to Ryker. His sharp eyes, his guarded expression, the way he looked at me tonight, like he was carrying the weight of the world on his shoulders.

Ryker's been through so much, more than anyone should have to endure. His mother, the one person who should have been his anchor, betrayed him. She turned her back on him, choosing her other son, Evander, instead. It's a pain I can't fully comprehend, but the thought of it twists something deep inside me.

I don't know what Ryker feels right now. Anger? Resentment? Or just emptiness? And then there's me—standing here, caught in my own web of questions and anger at my parents.

They've hidden so much from me, left me stumbling in the dark. I can't make sense of why they kept Neville's survival a secret, why they didn't tell me who I really am.

But as much as I'm drowning in my own turmoil, I can't stop thinking about Ryker. I feel a pang of guilt. He's been so steady, always there when I needed him, and now, when he needs someone the most, I'm lying here doing nothing.

I push the covers off and sit up, my feet brushing against the cool floor. My heart pounds as I glance over at Neville, still dead to the world. Slowly, I grab my hoodie from the back of the chair and slip it on, pulling the hood over my head. The air outside will be cold, but I'm too restless to care.

The door creaks softly as I open it, slipping out into the hallway. The Gothic architecture of Harlow Academy looms around me, its shadows stretching long and jagged under the pale moonlight. My sneakers make almost no sound on the stone floors as I make my way outside, the chilly night air biting at my skin.

I know exactly where I'm going—the garden. The place where I first met Ryker. That night feels like a lifetime ago, yet I remember every detail: the way the moonlight caught on his sharp features, the guarded curiosity in his gaze. Something about that moment had felt significant, like the universe had shifted slightly, aligning our paths.

The garden is quiet as I approach, the faint rustle of leaves in the breeze the only sound. The scent of earth and greenery fills the air, mingling with the faint sweetness of blooming flowers. I see him before he sees me, his tall figure silhouetted against the willow tree.

Ryker is leaning against the bench, his arms crossed, staring at the ground like it holds the answers to questions he hasn't even asked yet. His posture is tense, his shoulders rigid, and I can't help but wonder what's going through his mind.

"Couldn't sleep either, huh?" I say softly, stepping into the garden.

He looks up sharply, his eyes narrowing for a brief moment before relaxing. "Asterine," he says, his voice low. "What are you doing out here?"

"I could ask you the same thing," I reply, a small smile tugging at my lips.

He shrugs, pushing off the bench and shoving his hands into his jacket pockets. "Needed some air."

I walk closer, the grass crunching softly under my shoes. "So did I."

Ryker watches me for a moment before nodding toward the bench. "Sit," he says simply, and I do, settling onto the cool stone. He doesn't sit beside me but leans against the backrest, his gaze drifting upward to the sky.

The silence stretches between us, not uncomfortable but heavy with unspoken words. I watch him out of the corner of my eye, the way his jaw tightens, the faint crease between his brows. He looks tired—more than tired, really. Exhausted in a way that has nothing to do with sleep.

"I was thinking about you," I say, breaking the silence.

His head tilts slightly, his sharp eyes flicking to mine. "Oh yeah? What about me?"

"About... everything," I admit, my voice softer than I intended. "Your mom, what she did. How you've been handling it."

His expression hardens instantly, his walls snapping back into place. "I don't need your pity, Asterine."

"It's not pity," I say quickly, leaning forward. "It's... empathy,

I guess. I don't know what you're going through, but I can imagine how much it must hurt."

Ryker looks away, his jaw clenching. "It is what it is," he says flatly.

"No, it's not," I reply, my voice rising slightly. "She had no right to do that to you, Ryker. No right to treat you like—like you didn't matter."

He exhales sharply, running a hand through his dark hair. "She made her choice. Doesn't matter if I agree with it or not."

"But it does matter," I insist. "You matter, Ryker. Whether she sees that or not."

The words hang in the air between us, and for a moment, I think I've pushed him too far. But then he lets out a low, humorless laugh, shaking his head.

"You always this stubborn?" he asks, a faint smirk tugging at the corner of his lips.

"Always," I say, matching his smirk with one of my own.

He sits down beside me then, leaning forward with his elbows on his knees. For a long time, he doesn't say anything, and I don't push him. The sound of the wind rustling through the willow tree fills the silence, calming in its own way.

"You know what's funny?" he finally says, his voice quiet. "I don't even care that she picked Evander over me. What gets me is that she couldn't even tell me why. She didn't owe me much, but she owed me that."

I swallow hard, my chest tightening. "Maybe she was scared."

Ryker snorts. "Scared of what? Me?"

"Of losing you completely," I say. "Even if she didn't show it, maybe she thought pushing you away would hurt less than holding on and losing you anyway."

He's silent for a long moment, his gaze fixed on the ground.

"You think she misses me?"

I hesitate, unsure how to answer. "I think she should," I say finally.

Ryker exhales slowly, leaning back against the bench. The moonlight catches on his profile, highlighting the sharp angles of his face, the shadows under his eyes.

"Thanks, Asterine," he says after a while, his voice barely above a whisper.

"For what?"

"For being here," he replies simply.

I don't respond, but I don't need to. The tension in his posture has eased, his shoulders no longer hunched as if carrying the weight of the world. It's not much, but it's a start.

We sit there in silence, the garden around us alive with the soft hum of the night. The stars twinkle faintly above, distant and unreachable, but somehow comforting.

And for the first time in what feels like forever, I feel like we're both a little less alone.

# 6

# Normal Chaos

The shrill buzz of my alarm pulls me from sleep, and I groan, slapping the snooze button before Neville can complain again.

"Does it always sound like that?" he grumbles, sitting up on Eira's bed with his hair sticking out in every direction.

"Yes," I reply, sitting up and stretching. "And it's been two years, Neville, not two decades. Technology hasn't changed that much."

He scoffs, leaning back against the headboard. "Still feels weird, though. I mean, I'm technically not even supposed to be here, right?"

"Speaking of that," I say, glancing at the clock, "you've got a meeting with Dimick this morning, remember? You might want to put on something other than… whatever that is."

Neville looks down at his mismatched pajama pants and T-shirt. "What's wrong with this?"

"Everything," I reply, grabbing a hoodie from my chair. "Dimick's not exactly casual-Friday material."

Neville groans but gets up, rummaging through his bag for

something halfway decent.

"Relax," I add, smirking. "He's the one who has to figure out what to do with you, not the other way around."

"That's what I'm afraid of," he mutters, pulling on a sweater.

The classroom feels extra stuffy this morning, the windows fogged up from the chill outside. Mrs. Graham stands at the front, already jotting key themes from *Macbeth* on the whiteboard.

"Good morning, class," she says, her tone brisk. "I trust you've all read Act III by now?"

A chorus of mumbled affirmations ripples through the room as students shuffle into their seats. I sit near the middle, wedged between Eira and Jocosa, flipping open my notebook.

"Today, we'll focus on the theme of ambition," Mrs. Graham continues. "Macbeth's relentless desire for power ultimately leads to his downfall. Let's discuss."

The conversation flows around me, but my mind is elsewhere. Neville is probably in Dimick's office by now, explaining his "resurrection" and trying to convince the headmaster he's not a security risk. I can't help but feel a twinge of guilt for not being there, even though there's nothing I could do to help.

"Earth to Asterine," Eira whispers, nudging me with her elbow.

"Sorry," I mutter, focusing back on my notes.

"Stay with us," she says, smirking. "You're going to need this for the quiz on Friday."

The cafeteria is alive with noise—students shouting across tables, trays clattering, and the constant hum of overlapping conversations. I grab a plate of spaghetti and find our group in the usual corner booth.

Eira and Jocosa are deep in discussion about math homework, while Maeve is flipping through a history textbook, her lips moving as she mutters dates under her breath. Fabian is, predictably, doing nothing productive.

Neville arrives halfway through lunch, his expression unreadable as he slides into the seat beside me.

"Well?" I ask, raising an eyebrow.

He shrugs. "Dimick's still deciding. For now, I'm supposed to 'lay low.' Whatever that means."

"It means don't draw attention to yourself," Eira says, rolling her eyes. "Which, knowing you, is going to be impossible."

Neville smirks, stealing a piece of garlic bread from my plate. "I'll try my best."

Ryker shows up a moment later, dropping into the seat across from me. He looks tired, but not in a bad way—more like he's been up late working on something important.

"Morning," he says, grabbing a fry from Eira's plate.

"It's lunchtime," Jocosa corrects him.

"Details," Ryker replies, smirking.

The conversation quickly devolves into lighthearted bickering, with Neville throwing in sarcastic comments every chance he gets. For a moment, it feels almost normal—like we're just a group of friends navigating high school life instead of the tangled mess of secrets and paranormal drama that surrounds us.

The library is quieter than usual, the sound of pages turning and pens scratching filling the air. We've claimed a table in the corner, spreading out our books and notes in a chaotic mess.

Eira and Jocosa are hunched over their math assignments, whispering back and forth as they solve equations. Maeve is writing furiously in her notebook, her focus so intense it's almost intimidating.

Neville, of course, is doing absolutely nothing useful. He's lounging in a chair at the far end of the table, flipping through the calculator app on my phone like it's the most fascinating thing in the world.

"You know that's not how you do equations, right?" Jocosa says, glaring at him.

"Who said I was doing equations?" Neville replies, grinning.

"Then why are you here?" Eira snaps.

"To enjoy the ambiance," Neville says, leaning back in his chair.

Ryker chuckles, glancing up from his notebook. "Let him be. He's not bothering anyone."

"Yet," Jocosa mutters.

I try to focus on my history notes, but my mind keeps wandering. Between Dimick's expectations, my schoolwork, and the still-looming questions about my family, it's hard to keep everything straight.

"You okay?" Ryker asks, his voice low enough that only I can hear.

I glance at him and nod. "Yeah. Just… tired."

He doesn't press further, but the look in his eyes tells me he doesn't entirely believe me.

Back in the dorm, the weight of the day finally catches up to me. I collapse onto my bed, staring at the ceiling as the others gather around. Neville, predictably, looks completely unbothered, lounging on Eira's bed like it's his throne.

"Alright," I say, sitting up. "We need to figure this out."

"Figure what out?" Neville asks, feigning innocence.

"What to do with you," Eira snaps. "You've been dead for two years. You can't just walk around like nothing happened."

Neville shrugs. "Why not? People come back from vacations all the time. Call it an extended sabbatical."

"This isn't funny," Jocosa says, her tone sharp.

"Relax," Neville replies, sitting up. "Dimick said he'd handle it. Let him do his job."

"And in the meantime?" Maeve asks, crossing her arms.

"In the meantime, I'll stay out of trouble," Neville says with a smirk. "Mostly."

I groan, rubbing my temples. "This isn't a joke, Nev. People are going to notice you're… not dead."

He raises an eyebrow. "And you think I'm the one who has to explain that?"

"Yes," I reply, glaring at him. "You're the one who decided to come back."

"Technically, I didn't decide," he points out. "But fine. If it makes you feel better, I'll come up with a plan."

# 7

# Hey Roomie

The week has been nothing short of chaotic. The pressure of Headmaster Dimick's demands, the looming threat of failing the weekly tests, and the overwhelming sense that I'm being crushed under the weight of my own life have all piled up to this moment. The week had been nothing but endless hours of cramming, barely enough time to breathe, let alone think. And now, finally, it's here—test day.

It's still early morning when I walk into the grand hall for our weekly exams, feeling a tight knot in my stomach. The fluorescent lights buzz overhead, casting a cold, unwelcoming glow on the long rows of desks. Students are already seated, some of them staring blankly at the test papers in front of them, others fidgeting nervously, chewing the tips of their pens or drumming their fingers against the wood.

I feel a brief pang of sympathy for them—*for me*, honestly—but it vanishes as quickly as it came. I'm used to this by now. This pressure. This feeling like I'm about to crash into a brick wall and no one will be there to catch me.

At the very back of the room, Neville sits alone at a desk, tapping away at his phone. He's supposed to be in class, but for the past week, he's been taking it easy, working with Dimick on an alternative curriculum that lets him make up for the two years he was presumed dead. Dimick had finally agreed to let him stay at Harlow Academy—under the condition that he take on extra work for everything he'd missed. This meant late nights, extra assignments, and eventually transferring into a dorm room with Ryker.

Neville had been thrilled at first, mostly because it meant that he'd be closer to Ryker, his best mate from before his "death"—but the sudden shift to being a full-time student again, after two years of… not living, had left him feeling a bit out of place.

"Focus, Asterine," I mutter to myself, shaking my head to clear the thoughts. I don't have time to worry about Neville or his newly resurrected life. I can't afford to let my mind wander when there are tests waiting for me.

I take a deep breath and walk to my seat, settling down into the chair. The weight of the test papers in front of me is almost suffocating. But there's something else gnawing at my insides, something more unsettling than the fear of failing these stupid tests.

Neville and I were supposed to visit our parents today. It was supposed to be a chance for me to explain everything, to clear the air and tell them about what happened, about his return, about everything that's been going on. I had imagined the conversation a thousand times in my head, rehearsing the words, getting ready for the inevitable confrontation.

But of course, Neville had to fall sick.

I glance at him again across the room, sitting hunched over

his desk, his face pale and flushed, eyes glazed over. It's almost comical, in a way, how the universe seems determined to make my life as difficult as possible.

I sigh and open my test booklet. The questions blur in front of me, the words swimming on the page. I don't even know what subject this is anymore. My mind keeps drifting back to Neville, to his feverish state, and to the fact that we won't be visiting our parents today after all.

It's just another obstacle, I remind myself. Another thing I can't control, but still have to face.

I try to focus on the questions, scanning over them, but the pressure of everything weighs heavily on my shoulders. The test feels like an endless stretch of paper, one question after the other, and I can't seem to find my rhythm.

"Okay, just get through this," I whisper under my breath, my fingers tightening around the pencil.

The bell rings, signaling the end of the test. Students start packing up, the sound of pens clicking closed and papers rustling filling the air. I stand slowly, feeling like a zombie as I collect my things. I feel drained, like I've just run a marathon, but I haven't really gone anywhere.

Neville's still sitting at his desk, his face drawn, eyes heavy with exhaustion. He didn't even make it through the whole test. I knew he wouldn't.

"Hey, you okay?" I ask, walking over to him.

He looks up at me, blinking a few times as if trying to focus. "I'm fine. Just tired. Gonna sleep"

I don't believe him for a second. He looks like he's about to pass out, but I know he's not going to admit it. Not here, not now.

"I'll catch up with you later," I say, patting him on the shoulder. "Take it easy."

He gives me a half-smile, but it's weak, forced. "Yeah, sure."

I make my way out of the exam hall, my head spinning with everything that's happened. My parents, Neville's sudden fever, Ryker...

Ryker.

The thought of him makes my stomach go haywire for some reason.

When the day finally winds down and I return to the dorm, I find myself standing in the doorway for a moment, hesitating.

Neville and Ryker share a room now. It was the only option. Dimick had insisted that Neville integrate into the school, so he's been doing extra work—classwork from his previous years, as well as catching up on lessons with Ryker's help. We told him not to let our parents know anything because we ourselves wanted to tell them what all happened. That's the plan, anyway. It's still a bit surreal.

I don't know why it bothers me so much. But it does.

I walk in slowly, feeling like an intruder in a space that's already too familiar to them. Ryker's sitting on the edge of the bed, scrolling through something on his phone. Neville, on the other hand, is half-asleep, sprawled out on the other bed with his hands behind his head.

"You two are the picture of productivity," I say dryly, raising an eyebrow.

Ryker looks up at me and smirks. "What's the matter? Can't handle the slackers?"

I snort. "I'd have more energy if my life wasn't falling apart."

"Fair point," Neville mumbles from his bed. "But I can't help that I'm *sick*."

I narrow my eyes at him. "Sick, huh?"

"Yeah, sick," Neville says, pushing himself up and rubbing his temples. "I'm *dying* here."

Ryker chuckles. "You're dramatic. You were fine this morning."

"I'm not dramatic, I'm just *sensitive*," Neville retorts, his usual smugness returning.

I cross my arms. "You better be careful—Dimick will have you working extra hard to make up for that little break you're taking."

Neville groans. "Do I look like I care?"

Ryker looks at me and raises an eyebrow. "How's he doing, anyway?"

I glance at Neville, still looking like he's on the verge of passing out. "He's not doing great. He needs rest."

Ryker sighs, rubbing the back of his neck. "He's got a lot to catch up on. But he's making progress. I'll get him up to speed."

I watch him closely, my thoughts swirling. Something about this—about them—feels… different. Something in the air feels thick, charged with unspoken tension. Ryker's dark eyes seem to pierce through me in a way that makes my heart skip a beat.

His midnight black eyes lock onto mine, and for a split second, I feel like the ground beneath me has shifted. His copper tousled hair falls in messy waves around his face, and I can't help but trace the sharp lines of his jaw—strong enough to cut steel. There's a pull between us, subtle but undeniable, and it's as if the entire room falls away.

"Are you alright?" he asks, his voice low, laced with something I can't quite identify.

I blink, startled by the intensity of his gaze. "Yeah, I'm fine,"

I say, forcing a smile. My voice is steady, but inside, my mind is racing.

For a moment, the air between us crackles. I can feel it, that spark, that energy we've always had, but now it feels stronger, charged with something deeper, something neither of us has acknowledged before.

I open my mouth to say something, anything, but the moment passes too quickly. Ryker stands up, his tall frame moving effortlessly as he grabs his jacket from the chair.

"You should probably go," he says, his voice quieter now, but the underlying tension still hangs between us like an invisible thread.

I don't respond right away. I just nod, my throat tight, and turn to leave.

As I walk out of the room, I feel his gaze still lingering on me, pulling at me, and I wonder how long I can ignore this strange pull between us.

# 8

# Blood-red Moon

The room is dark and still, save for the soft sound of Eira's even breathing beside me. She's sound asleep, her chest rising and falling in a soothing rhythm that should calm me, but it doesn't.

I'm lying on my back, staring at the ceiling, my thoughts spiraling in endless loops. The events of the day churn in my mind like a storm I can't escape—Neville's fever, the weekly tests, Ryker.

Ryker.

I close my eyes, but it only makes the memories sharper. His midnight black eyes, so intense and probing, as if he could see every hidden part of me. The way his copper hair fell messily around his face, catching the dim light in a way that made it impossible not to notice. And that jaw—sharp enough to cut steel, just like the edge in his voice when he spoke.

I shake my head, trying to push the thoughts away. *Why can't I stop thinking about him?*

Beside me, Eira stirs slightly, murmuring something incoherent before settling back into her peaceful slumber. She looks so calm, so unbothered, and for a moment, I envy her. How does she do it? How does she shut out the noise, the chaos, the constant weight of everything?

I sigh softly, turning onto my side to face the wall. My chest feels tight, like the air in the room is too thick, too heavy to breathe. The walls seem to press in around me, the shadows growing darker and more oppressive.

It's suffocating.

I can't stay here.

Careful not to wake Eira, I slip out of bed, grabbing my hoodie from the chair and pulling it on as I quietly open the door. The hallway is dimly lit, the flickering sconces casting long, dancing shadows on the stone walls.

The air is cooler out here, but it doesn't do much to ease the tightness in my chest. I start walking, my footsteps echoing softly on the stone floor. The Gothic architecture of Harlow Academy looms around me, the intricate patterns on the walls and the towering arches above casting an almost otherworldly aura.

The tapestries hanging along the hallway catch my attention. They're ancient, their colors faded but still vibrant enough to depict strange, surreal scenes—battles between winged creatures and armored knights, forests filled with glowing eyes, shadowy figures standing in circles of fire.

I run my fingers along the edge of one tapestry, the fabric rough against my skin. "What kind of world is this?" I whisper to myself.

The thought sends a shiver down my spine. This school isn't just a place for learning. It's a crossroads—a place where the supernatural and the mundane collide. And even though I've been here for weeks, I still don't understand the full extent of what that means.

What else is out there? What creatures walk among us, hidden in plain sight?

I shake my head, trying to clear the thoughts. The air feels heavy again, like it's pressing down on me, making it hard to breathe.

Then I hear it.

A soft *swish*, like something fast and light moving just behind me.

I freeze, my heart skipping a beat. Slowly, I turn around, my eyes scanning the hallway. The flickering light from the sconces casts shifting shadows on the walls, but there's nothing there.

"Hello?" I call out, my voice barely above a whisper.

Silence.

I wait, every muscle in my body tense, but the hallway remains empty. Just shadows and silence.

"Get a grip, Asterine," I mutter under my breath. "You're sleep-deprived, that's all."

Still, I can't shake the feeling that I'm not alone.

By the time I make it back to my room, the eerie sensation has faded, replaced by a dull ache of exhaustion. I close the door quietly behind me, leaning against it for a moment as I take a deep breath.

The room is just as I left it—dark and quiet, with Eira's soft breathing filling the silence. But something feels… off.

My gut twists uncomfortably, and I glance around the room, my eyes lingering on the shadows in the corners. Nothing's out of place, but the unease won't go away.

I walk slowly toward my bed, my gaze drifting to Eira. She's lying on her side, her back to me, the blankets pulled up to her shoulders.

"Eira?" I whisper, my voice trembling slightly.

No response.

My chest tightens as the unease turns into full-blown fear. My heart races, pounding in my ears as I step closer.

"Eira," I say again, louder this time. Still nothing.

I reach out, my hand trembling as I touch her shoulder.

She doesn't move.

I take another step closer, leaning over her to see her face. And that's when I see it.

The scream rips from my throat before I can stop it, echoing through the room like a shattered mirror.

Eira's face is pale, her eyes half-closed, her lips slightly parted. Blood pools beneath her neck, staining the pillow and seeping into the sheets. It's dark and thick, spreading like a grotesque halo around her head.

My legs give out, and I collapse to my knees beside the bed, my hands shaking violently.

# 9

## Sucker blood

"No," I whisper, my voice breaking. "No, no, no…"

My chest heaves as panic overtakes me, but a sliver of determination cuts through the terror. I lean forward, my hands trembling as I place them on Eira's shoulders.

"Come on, Eira. Stay with me," I murmur, my voice cracking.

I gently turn her over to face me, and that's when I see it—the source of the blood. A wound, jagged and raw, mars the side of her neck, hidden just beneath her hairline. The blood pools thickly around it, the crimson against her pale skin making my stomach churn.

My breath catches in my throat. I don't know how deep it is or what caused it, but I know one thing: she's still alive. Her chest rises and falls, faint but steady.

I grab my handkerchief from my bedside table, pressing it firmly against the wound to stem the bleeding. My hand shakes as I hold it there, trying to keep the pressure steady. With my free hand, I fumble for my phone, my fingers slipping over the screen as I scroll to Ryker's name.

The line rings once, twice, and then his voice comes through, sharp and alert.

"Asterine? What's going on?"

"Ryker," I gasp, my voice trembling with urgency. "It's Eira—she's hurt. I need you. Now."

He doesn't hesitate. "On my way. Stay with her."

The line goes dead, and I toss the phone aside, my attention back on Eira. Her skin feels cold under my hand, her breathing too shallow for comfort.

"Hang on, Eira," I whisper, willing her to hold on. "Ryker's coming. You're going to be okay."

Minutes later, the door bursts open, and Ryker strides in, his copper tousled hair disheveled, his midnight black eyes scanning the room with laser focus.

"What happened?" he demands, crossing the room in two long strides.

"I don't know," I reply, my voice shaky. "I found her like this. We need to get her to the medical room. Now."

Ryker doesn't waste time asking more questions. He gently lifts Eira from the bed, his arms steady despite the urgency in his movements. "Let's go," he says, his tone clipped but calm.

I follow close behind as we rush through the dimly lit hallways of Harlow Academy. The shadows on the walls seem to stretch and shift as we move, and I can't shake the feeling that we're being watched. But I push the thought aside, focusing on Eira's limp form in Ryker's arms.

The medical room is quiet, the sterile smell of antiseptic filling the air as we burst through the doors. The nurse, a stern-looking woman with sharp eyes and a no-nonsense demeanor, looks up from her desk, startled.

"What happened?" she asks, rising to her feet.

"She's bleeding," Ryker says, his voice steady. "Neck wound. We don't know how it happened."

The nurse gestures to an examination bed. "Put her down here. Quickly."

Ryker lays Eira on the bed, and the nurse immediately goes to work, her hands moving with practiced efficiency. She grabs gauze, antiseptic, and surgical scissors, cutting away the blood-soaked fabric around the wound.

"Wait outside," she orders without looking up.

"But—" I begin, my voice rising in protest.

"Out," she snaps, her tone brooking no argument.

Reluctantly, Ryker and I step into the waiting area just outside the room. The silence between us is heavy, filled with unspoken questions and tension. How in the hell did that happen to her and why would someone do something like that? How did they even enter in our dorm. I should have stayed back in there, I shouldn't have gone outside at all. I could have prevented this but its now all in vain.

I pace back and forth, my arms crossed tightly over my chest. Ryker leans against the wall, his expression unreadable, but I can feel the tension radiating off him.

"What do you think happened?" I ask, breaking the silence.

He shakes his head. "I don't know. But whatever it was, it wasn't normal."

I stop pacing, turning to face him. "You think this was... supernatural?"

"Don't you?" he counters, his midnight eyes locking onto mine. "This is Harlow. Weird things don't just happen—they're usually caused."

I don't respond, but the weight of his words settles heavily on my shoulders. He's right. This place is a magnet for the strange and unexplainable, and Eira's injury feels like just another piece of a much larger, darker puzzle.

The nurse finally emerges, wiping her hands on a cloth. "She's stable," she says, with a brisk tone.

Relief floods through me, but it's quickly overshadowed by the burning need for answers. "What happened to her?" I demand, stepping forward.

The nurse's sharp eyes fix on me. "How did you find her?"

I blink, caught off guard by the question. "I—I couldn't sleep. I left the room to get some air, and when I came back, I saw the blood."

The nurse nods slowly, her eyes unreadable. Then she turns to Ryker. "Come inside. Both of you."

We exchange a glance before following her back into the medical room. Eira lies on the bed, pale but breathing steadily. The bandage on her neck is stark against her skin, a grim reminder of how close she came to...

No. I can't let my mind go there.

The nurse walks to Eira's side and carefully begins unwrapping the bandage. "I think you should see this," she says quietly.

As the last layer of gauze falls away, I feel Ryker stiffen beside me. His sharp intake of breath is loud in the otherwise silent room.

"Oh my god," he mutters, his voice barely audible.

My eyes dart to the wound, and what I see makes want to run away. It's not a cut, not exactly. The edges of the wound are jagged, almost burnt-looking, as if something sharp and hot had pierced her skin. But that's not what makes my blood run cold.

Two puncture marks sit at the center of the wound, perfectly spaced, oozing faint traces of blood.

My heart pounds in my chest, my breath catching in my throat. "What… what is that?" I whisper.

The nurse meets my stare, her expression grim. "That's what I was hoping you could tell me."

# 10

# New-old life

The nurse's voice hangs in the air, her words cutting through the sterile silence of the medical room.

"It's a vampire bite."

For a moment, I can't breathe. The words seem to echo endlessly, bouncing off the walls and pressing against my chest. My gaze shifts to Eira, lying pale and unconscious on the bed, the stark white bandage on her neck hiding the source of the blood that had pooled beneath her just hours ago.

"No," I whisper, shaking my head. My voice cracks under the weight of my disbelief. "That's not possible. It… it can't be."

The nurse folds her arms, her sharp eyes meeting mine. "It's possible, Miss Ashworth. It's reality. She's been bitten by a vampire, and the transformation has already started."

The word transformation hits me like a physical blow. My knees feel weak, and I stumble slightly, catching myself on the edge of the examination table.

"What does that even mean?" I ask, my voice trembling. "What transformation?"

Ryker shifts uncomfortably beside me, and I glance at him. His usually confident posture is gone, replaced by something almost defensive. His midnight black eyes dart briefly to the nurse before settling on the floor.

"She's turning into one of them," the nurse says bluntly.

The air seems to grow colder, heavier. I can't comprehend what she's saying. My mind races, trying to piece together some explanation, some way this could all be a mistake.

"No," I say again, louder this time. "There has to be another explanation. Eira isn't… she can't…" My voice falters, and I feel tears pricking at the corners of my eyes.

"There's no mistake," the nurse says, her tone firm but not unkind. "The signs are clear. She's been bitten, and there's no cure for that."

My breath catches, and I force myself to look at Eira again. Her pale face is almost unrecognizable, her usual lively complexion replaced by something ghostly. She's always been full of energy, quick-witted and sharp-tongued, the kind of person who could find humor in the darkest of situations.

But now she looks fragile, as if the slightest touch could break her.

"How long?" Ryker's voice breaks the silence.

The nurse hesitates, her sharp gaze shifting to him. "It varies. Days, weeks. It depends on her strength and her ability to resist the hunger."

Hunger. The word sends a shiver down my spine.

"What do you mean, resist?" I ask, stepping closer to the nurse. "What hunger?"

She sighs, as if bracing herself for what she's about to say. "The hunger for blood. It's part of the transformation. As the change progresses, she'll start craving it. At first, she might be able to control it, but eventually…" She trails off, her expression grim.

"Eventually what?" I press, my voice rising.

"She won't be able to resist," the nurse says softly. "And if she can't feed…" She doesn't finish the sentence, but the implication is clear.

I feel my stomach churn, bile rising in my throat. I want to scream, to demand answers, to find someone to blame.

"We can't just let this happen," I say, turning to Ryker. My voice is desperate, pleading. "There has to be something we can do. A spell, a potion, anything."

Ryker doesn't meet my eyes. His jaw is clenched, his hands balled into fists at his sides. "There's nothing," he says finally, his voice low and tight.

I stare at him, the weight of his words sinking in. "You're lying," I say, shaking my head. "There has to be something. We can't just… just let her turn into one of them!"

The nurse steps between us, her expression stern. "You need to calm down, Miss Ashworth. Your friend needs support, not hysteria."

"Hysteria?" I repeat, my voice cracking. "You're telling me my best friend is turning into a vampire, and you expect me to be calm?"

The nurse doesn't flinch. "If you want to help her, you'll need to be strong. She's going to need you in the days ahead."

Her words sting, but I know she's right. I swallow hard, forcing myself to take a deep breath.

"What do I do?" I ask, my voice barely above a whisper.

The nurse's gaze softens slightly. "For now, keep her close. Watch for changes—sensitivity to light, heightened senses, mood swings. And when the hunger starts…" She hesitates.

"You'll have to decide how far you're willing to go to help her."

I don't respond. I can't.

"Now if you'll excuse me, I have to report this incident to The Headmaster" she says and goes inside her cabin where I watch her dial numbers into the telephone.

When Ryker and I leave the medical room, the tension between us is palpable. We walk in silence through the dimly lit hallways of Harlow Academy, the flickering sconces casting long shadows on the walls.

"You knew," I say finally, my voice low but accusing.

Ryker stops, turning to face me. "I suspected," he admits, his midnight black eyes meeting mine.

"And you didn't think to tell me?" My voice rises, trembling with anger. "You just let me walk into that room without a clue what was happening?"

"What would you have done if I had told you?" he asks, his tone sharper than I expected. "Would it have changed anything? Would it have made it easier to hear?"

I open my mouth to respond, but the words die in my throat. I hate that he's right.

"Look," Ryker says, his voice softening. "I know this is hard, but we'll figure it out. Eira's strong. She can handle this."

"And what if she can't?" I ask, my voice barely above a whisper.

Ryker doesn't answer.

# 11

# Revelation

The faint light of morning seeps through the curtains, casting a grayish glow across the medical room. I'm slumped in a chair by Eira's bed, my head heavy in my hands, my thoughts an endless loop of fear and helplessness.

The sound of rustling pulls me from my stupor, and I lift my head. Eira is stirring.

Her eyelids flutter, her lips parting as she lets out a faint groan. Slowly, her eyes open, their usual vibrant blue now dulled and tired. She looks around the room, her gaze unfocused, before landing on me.

"Asterine?" she whispers, her voice hoarse.

I'm at her side in an instant, relief flooding through me. "Eira! You're awake."

She blinks at me, her brows furrowing in confusion. "What... what happened? Where am I?"

"You're in the medical room," I say softly, brushing a strand of hair from her face. "You're safe."

Her hand moves to her neck, her fingers brushing against the bandage. She winces, her eyes widening. "What... why does it hurt?"

I swallow hard, glancing at the nurse, who stands silently by the door. Turning back to Eira, I force myself to speak. "Eira, something happened last night. I—"

"What happened?" she interrupts, her voice rising with panic. She tries to sit up, but I gently push her back down.

"Hey, hey, take it easy," I say, my voice as soothing as I can manage. "You're okay. Just breathe."

She shakes her head, tears welling in her eyes. "No, I'm not okay! Asterine, what's going on? Why am I here?"

I hesitate, my chest tightening. How am I supposed to tell her? How do I even begin to explain what happened?

"Eira," I say slowly, "you were hurt last night. There was… an incident."

She stares at me, her breathing shallow. "What kind of incident?"

I glance at the nurse again, hoping for some guidance, but she remains silent, her expression unreadable.

"You were bitten," I say finally, my voice trembling. "By… by something."

Her brows furrow in confusion. "Bitten? What do you mean, bitten? By what?"

I take a deep breath, steadying myself. "By a vampire."

For a moment, the room is silent, the weight of my words hanging in the air.

Eira stares at me, her expression shifting from confusion to disbelief. "A vampire?" she repeats, her voice barely above a whisper. "You're joking, right?"

"I wish I were," I say, my throat tightening.

She shakes her head, her hands trembling. "No. No, that's not possible. Vampires aren't real. They're not—"

"They are," I cut in gently. "And you were bitten by one."

Her breathing quickens, panic flickering in her eyes. "No. No, that's insane. You're lying."

"I'm not lying," I say firmly. "I swear, Eira. This is real. And…" I hesitate, the next words catching in my throat. "And it's changing you."

Eira stares at me, her chest rising and falling rapidly. "Changing me? What are you talking about?"

"The bite," I say softly. "It's… it's turning you into one of them."

Her face pales, and she looks down at her hands, as if expecting them to change before her eyes. "No," she whispers. "That's not possible. I'd remember. I'd know if something like that happened to me."

I glance at the nurse, who steps forward. "Memory loss isn't uncommon in cases like this," she says calmly. "The trauma of the bite, combined with the transformation, can create gaps in recollection."

Eira shakes her head again, tears streaming down her cheeks. "No, this isn't happening. This can't be happening."

"Eira," I say, reaching for her hand. "Please, try to remember. Do you recall anything from last night? Anything strange, anything unusual?"

She squeezes her eyes shut, her hands clenching into fists. For a long moment, she says nothing, her breath hitching as she struggles to think.

Finally, she opens her eyes, her expression pained. "I… I don't remember," she says, her voice trembling. "I don't remember anything."

The knot in my stomach tightens, and I feel the weight of the situation settle even heavier on my shoulders.

"You don't have to remember right now," I say gently. "But you need to trust me, Eira. We'll figure this out together."

Her eyes meet mine, and for a moment, she looks like the Eira I've always known—scared, vulnerable, but still fighting. "What's going to happen to me?" she asks, her voice barely audible.

The nurse answers before I can. "The transformation has begun," she says, her tone clinical but firm. "Over the next few days, you'll start to experience changes—heightened senses, aversion to sunlight, and most significantly, an uncontrollable thirst for blood."

Eira recoils, horror etched into her features. "No," she whispers, shaking her head. "No, I don't want that. I don't want to be… to be one of them."

I squeeze her hand tightly, my own tears threatening to spill. "We'll find a way, Eira. We'll figure something out."

"There is no cure," the nurse says bluntly, and my head snaps toward her, anger flaring in my chest.

"Stop saying that!" I snap, my voice trembling with frustration. "There has to be something. There has to be a way to stop this."

The nurse shakes her head, her expression unyielding. "I'm sorry, Miss Ashworth. But there isn't. The only thing you can do now is help her manage it."

By the time Eira is cleared to return to our dorm, night has fallen. The walk back is quiet, the shadows in the hallways seeming longer, darker than usual. Eira leans on me heavily, her steps slow and unsteady.

When we finally reach our room, she collapses onto her bed without a word, her back to me.

"Eira," I say softly, sitting on the edge of my own bed. "Do you need anything? Water? Food?"

She shakes her head, her voice muffled. "Just... leave me alone."

Her words sting, but I don't push her. I lie down, staring at the ceiling, my mind racing. How am I supposed to help her? What am I supposed to do?

The next morning, Eira barely speaks. She sits on the edge of her bed, her eyes distant, her shoulders slumped.

I bring her a plate from the dining hall—eggs, toast, and fruit—and set it on the table between us. "You should eat," I say gently.

She looks at the plate, her nose wrinkling in distaste. "I'm not hungry," she mutters.

"You didn't eat anything yesterday," I press. "You need your strength."

She picks up a piece of toast, taking a small bite before grimacing and setting it down. "It tastes... wrong," she says, her voice barely above a whisper.

I frown, watching her closely. "Wrong how?"

She shrugs, avoiding my gaze. "Just... wrong. Like it's not real."

My chest tightens, and I glance at the bandage on her neck. The nurse's warnings echo in my mind.

"It's the hunger," she had said. "It's already starting."

By the time the sun sets again, Eira is even quieter, her usual fire extinguished. She spends most of the day in bed, staring blankly at the ceiling or sleeping fitfully.

I sit by her side, reading, studying, anything to keep myself occupied. But every so often, I glance at her, my heart aching.

This isn't Eira.

This is someone else.

And as much as I want to believe I can save her, a small, horrible voice in the back of my mind whispers that I might already be too late.

## 12

# A Plan

T he door creaks open as Neville steps into the dimly lit dorm room, his eyes scanning every corner before landing on Eira. She's sitting on the edge of her bed, her hands folded tightly in her lap, her posture rigid. Her pale face glows faintly under the overhead light, but there's something different about her now—something sharper, more unsettling.

I sit beside her, my heart heavy with guilt and uncertainty. The room feels suffocating, the tension palpable as Maeve, Fabian, Jocosa, and Headmaster Dimick file in one by one. The air is thick with unspoken questions, their faces etched with a mix of curiosity and concern. But my gaze hovers to the door, waiting for Ryker to come in too. I don't know why I have been wanting to see him but I haven't had a proper chance to talk to him since last night. I should probably thank him for coming to rescue and taking Eira to the medical room.

Dimick shuts the door behind him, his dark robes trailing the floor as he surveys the room. His usually composed demeanor is replaced by something sterner, more serious. No Ryker then

I guess; Or maybe he would come later? Where even is he and why isn't he not here when everybody else is?

"Eira," Dimick begins, his voice low but firm. "How are you feeling?"

Eira hesitates, her fingers tightening around the fabric of her skirt. "Different," she says finally, her voice barely above a whisper. "It's like... everything is sharper. Louder. But also harder to control."

Everyone exchanges glances, the weight of her words sinking in. Maeve is the first to break the silence, stepping forward with her arms crossed. "So it's true, then? She's... a vampire now?"

Dimick nods slowly. "The signs are clear. Whoever attacked her didn't just feed—they turned her."

The words hit me like a punch to the gut. I glance at Eira, who looks down, her expression a mix of fear and shame.

"I don't understand," Fabian says, his voice tinged with frustration. "Why would a rogue vampire do this? What's the point?"

Dimick's expression darkens. "Rogue vampires don't follow rules or reason. They act on instinct, hunger, and often orders from more sinister sources. We need to find out who did this and why before anyone else gets hurt."

Jocosa sits on the arm of a nearby chair, her fingers absent-mindedly tracing patterns in the fabric. "Do you think it's someone from outside the Academy?" she asks, her voice thoughtful. "Or... could it be one of the vampires here?"

A chill runs down my spine at the suggestion. The idea that someone we've seen in the hallways, someone we might've shared a meal or a class with, could be responsible for this is terrifying.

"We can't rule anything out," Dimick replies, his tone grim. "Which is why I'll be calling a meeting with all the vampire students. We need answers, and we need them now."

"I don't even remember what happened," Eira says suddenly, her voice trembling. All eyes turn to her as she looks up, tears brimming in her eyes. "One moment I was walking back to the dorms, and the next… everything went black. When I woke up, I was here, and everything was… different."

Neville steps closer to her, his face a mixture of concern and determination. "We'll figure this out," he says firmly. "Whoever did this is going to pay."

His words hang in the air, a promise that feels both comforting and ominous.

As the conversation continues, I feel myself sinking deeper into my thoughts. Guilt claws at my chest, each word a reminder of how I failed to protect Eira. She's my best friend, and I couldn't save her.

What if I had stayed with her that night? What if I had sensed the danger earlier? Would she still be the same Eira, the same girl who used to laugh at my jokes and share late-night snacks in our dorm?

"Ash?" Maeve's voice pulls me from my spiraling thoughts.

I look up to find everyone staring at me, their expressions expectant. "What?"

"I asked if you've noticed anything strange," Maeve says, her tone laced with curiosity. "Anything that might help us figure out who did this."

I shake my head, swallowing the lump in my throat. "No. I haven't."

Dimick straightens, his gaze sweeping across the room. "Until we get to the bottom of this, I want everyone to be vigilant. No wandering around alone, especially after dark. And Eira…"

He turns to her, his expression softening slightly. "You're going to need guidance. Adjusting to this new… existence won't be easy, but we'll help you through it."

Eira nods, her eyes downcast. "Thank you."

Dimick's gaze lingers on her for a moment before he turns to the rest of us. "I'll see you all tomorrow. Be ready for the meeting."

With that, he leaves the room, his presence lingering like a shadow.

As the door clicks shut behind him, the room descends into an uneasy silence. Fabian shifts uncomfortably, his usual confidence replaced by something quieter, more subdued.

"This is messed up," he mutters, running a hand through his hair.

"No kidding," Maeve replies, her tone sharp. "But sitting around feeling sorry for ourselves isn't going to help. We need to figure out what's going on."

Neville nods, his jaw tight. "And we will. But for now, Eira needs rest."

He looks at me, his gaze steady. "Ash, stay with her tonight. Make sure she's okay."

I nod, the weight of responsibility settling heavily on my shoulders.

Later, as I sit by Eira's bedside, watching her drift off to sleep, I can't help but feel the crushing weight of everything that's happened.

How did we get here? Just a few weeks ago, our biggest concern was passing our exams. Now, we're dealing with rogue vampires, life-altering transformations, and secrets I can barely begin to unravel.

As I sit in the dimly lit room, the soft sound of Eira's breathing filling the silence, one thought keeps repeating in my mind:

This is just the beginning.

# 13

# Ultimatum

The grand assembly hall looms before me, its tall arched windows casting streaks of moonlight across the cold stone floor. The room is eerily silent save for the faint rustle of cloaks and the shuffling of hesitant footsteps as the vampire students gather.

Dimick stands at the front, his dark silhouette framed by the faint glow of enchanted lanterns that line the walls. His presence dominates the space, his sharp gaze sweeping over the gathering like a hawk surveying prey.

I hang back near the doorway, my arms crossed tightly over my chest. Why do I feel like a spectator to my own nightmare? The tension in the air is suffocating, every breath heavy with unspoken accusations and rising fear.

One by one, the vampire students take their places. Only ten of them. A small group, but their collective aura is overwhelming—cold, sharp, and impossibly unsettling. Each movement, each glance, feels deliberate, calculated.

Someone speaks, breaking the oppressive silence. "Where's Ryker?"

The question cuts through the room like a knife, drawing every gaze toward the speaker—a tall boy with jet-black hair and piercing green eyes. Caelan. His voice is steady, but there's a note of suspicion, of challenge, in his tone.

I stiffen at the mention of Ryker's name, my heart skipping a beat. I hadn't noticed his absence until now. My eyes dart around the room, searching for his familiar figure, but he's nowhere to be seen.

Dimick's expression doesn't falter. "Ryker is not our concern at the moment," he says firmly, his voice brooking no argument.

But the words do nothing to quell the unease rising in my chest. Where is he? Why wouldn't he be here for something this important?

Dimick steps forward, his dark robes trailing behind him like shadows. "Let's begin," he says, his voice low and commanding.

The room falls silent, the weight of his authority settling over us like a heavy blanket.

"Last night, one of our students was attacked," Dimick begins, his gaze sharp as it sweeps over the group. "Eira. She has survived, but she is forever changed. She has been turned."

The murmurs start immediately, low and disbelieving, but they grow louder with each passing second.

"Turned?" A girl near the back exclaims, her voice rising in panic. "That's impossible! No one here would—"

"Silence!" Dimick's voice cracks through the air like a whip, and the murmurs cease instantly.

His gaze hardens, his expression colder than I've ever seen it. "This was not an accident. It was deliberate. And whoever is responsible is not only a danger to Eira but to everyone in this Academy."

The group shifts uncomfortably, glancing at one another with suspicion. The tension is almost tangible, the air thick with distrust.

"You're accusing us?" Caelan speaks again, his tone laced with defiance. "We've done nothing wrong. If a rogue vampire is responsible, that's your problem, Dimick—not ours."

Dimick's gaze locks onto him, unflinching. "A rogue vampire may have committed the act, but rogues don't act without reason or direction. If someone here knows something, now is the time to speak."

The weight of his words settles over the room, and I can feel the unease ripple through the group.

I shift uncomfortably, my back pressed against the cold stone wall. My heart is pounding, my thoughts a chaotic whirlwind. Why Eira? Why now? And who would do something like this?

The room feels suffocating, the tension pressing down on me like a vice. I glance around, watching the vampires' reactions. Some look angry, their pride wounded by Dimick's accusations. Others... others look nervous.

Is it guilt? Fear? Or something else entirely?

I bite my lip, the unease gnawing at me. And then, like an uninvited whisper in my mind, a thought surfaces. Where is Ryker?

"You have until the end of the week," Dimick announces, his voice cutting through the silence like a blade. "If the culprit is among you and does not come forward, I will take measures to uncover the truth myself."

The air grows heavier, the weight of his words settling like a storm cloud.

"What kind of measures?" Alina asks, her voice trembling.

Dimick doesn't answer immediately. Instead, he lets the

silence stretch, the tension crackling like static electricity. Finally, he speaks, his voice quiet but lethal. "Measures you won't enjoy."

The room erupts into chaos.

"You can't do that!" Caelan shouts, his fists clenched. "You have no right to treat us like criminals!"

"This is absurd!" another vampire exclaims. "You're punishing us for something we didn't do!"

Through it all, Eira sits quietly near the front, her head bowed, her hands gripping the edge of her seat. She hasn't spoken a word since the meeting began, her pale face etched with exhaustion and something deeper—fear, maybe? Or shame?

Dimick turns to her, his expression softening slightly. "Eira," he says gently. "Do you remember anything about the attack? Anything at all?"

Eira hesitates, her fingers tightening around the fabric of her skirt. "No," she whispers, her voice trembling. "I don't remember anything. Just... darkness."

Her words hang in the air, heavy and unrelenting.

"You'll be part of this investigation," Dimick says, his tone firm but kind. "Your perspective may help us uncover the truth."

Eira nods slowly, but her eyes remain fixed on the floor.

I feel a lump rise in my throat as I watch her. She looks so small, so fragile—so unlike the Eira I've always known.

This is my fault. I should've been there. I should've protected her.

The thought tears at me, a gnawing guilt that refuses to be silenced.

Dimick steps back, his gaze sweeping over the group one

final time. "You all know what's at stake. Don't make me regret trusting you."

With that, the meeting is over. The vampires file out of the hall, their murmurs filling the air like a low hum.

Eira lingers, her shoulders slumped, her eyes downcast. I move to her side, placing a hand on her arm. "Are you okay?"

She looks up at me, her eyes glistening with unshed tears. "I don't know, Ash," she says softly. "I just... I don't know."

# 14

# Bondings

The sun filters through the curtains of the dorm room, casting streaks of light across the floor. The air is thick with an unspoken tension, a weight that seems to cling to everything since Eira's transformation. I sit on my bed, my back pressed against the wall, watching as Neville and Eira occupy the small space near the window.

Eira leans against the sill, her arms crossed tightly over her chest, her gaze fixed on the courtyard below. Her usually bright eyes seem duller now, as though the light has been drained from them. Neville stands beside her, his posture stiff, his expression unreadable.

I glance between them, my thoughts swirling. It's strange, seeing them like this. Eira, so unsure of herself, and Neville, so… steady. Protective.

"You don't have to stay here, you know," Eira says suddenly, her voice breaking the heavy silence. She doesn't turn to look at Neville, but her tone carries a mix of irritation and vulnerability. "I'm fine."

Neville raises an eyebrow, his lips twitching into the faintest hint of a smile. "Fine? Sure. That's why you're standing there looking like you're about to jump out the window."

Eira turns to glare at him, but there's no real heat behind it. "I'm serious, Neville. You don't have to babysit me."

"I'm not babysitting," he replies, leaning casually against the wall. "I'm supervising. Big difference."

I can't help but smirk at their exchange. It's a small moment, but it feels… normal. Almost like nothing's changed.

But everything has changed. Eira isn't the same, and neither are any of us.

Still, watching Neville's calm, teasing demeanor seems to put her at ease, even if she won't admit it.

Eira sighs, running a hand through her hair. "I don't feel fine," she mutters, her voice barely audible. "I feel… wrong. Like I don't even know who I am anymore."

Neville's teasing smile fades, replaced by something softer. He steps closer, his voice quiet but firm. "You're still you, Eira. Being a vampire doesn't change who you are. It just adds… complications."

Eira lets out a bitter laugh. "Complications? That's one way to put it."

Neville shrugs. "Well, if anyone can handle complications, it's you."

For a moment, Eira just looks at him, her expression unreadable. Then, to my surprise, she smiles—a small, hesitant smile, but a smile nonetheless.

I look away, my fingers curling around the edge of my blanket. Why can't I do that? Why can't I make her feel better like Neville does? She's my best friend, and I'm just sitting here, useless.

The thought gnaws at me, a sharp ache that refuses to be

ignored.

"So," Neville says, his tone lighter now. "Have you tried any… vampire stuff yet? Super speed? Strength? Climbing walls?"

Eira snorts, rolling her eyes. "What do you think I am? A Marvel superhero?"

Neville grins. "I don't know. You could at least try the wall thing. Might be fun."

Eira shakes her head, but her smile lingers. "You're ridiculous."

"That's what they tell me," Neville replies, his grin widening.

"Any new cravings? Blood smoothies? Plasma popsicles?"

Eira snorts again, the sound breaking the heaviness in the room. "Gross. And no, thanks for asking."

"Just checking," Neville replies, grinning. "Wouldn't want you sneaking into the kitchen at night and terrifying the cooks."

Eira rolls her eyes, but there's a hint of amusement in her expression. "If I ever get that desperate, you'll be the first to know."

"Alright, you two," I say, finally breaking my silence. "If you're done with the comedy routine, maybe we can figure out what to do next."

Eira glances at me, raising an eyebrow. "Next? What do you mean?"

I shrug. "I mean, you're a vampire now. That's not exactly something we can ignore. You're going to need, I don't know… a plan. A schedule. Something to keep you from losing it."

Neville chuckles. "You make her sound like she's a ticking time bomb."

I shoot him a look. "She kind of is, isn't she?"

Eira groans, running a hand over her face. "Great. I'm a ticking time bomb. Thanks for the confidence boost, Ash."

"Okay, but seriously," I say, leaning forward. "What's the plan? You can't just sit around moping forever."

"I'm not moping," Eira protests, though her tone lacks conviction.

"Sure, you're not," Neville says, smirking. "That's why you've been staring out the window like a sad movie character for the past hour."

Eira glares at him, but there's no real anger in her eyes. "Fine. What do you suggest, oh wise one?"

Neville leans back, crossing his arms. "Simple. You figure out what you need. Blood, control, all that fun stuff. And we'll help you. Right, Ash?"

I nod, though a small part of me hesitates. Can we really help her? Can I?

"Great," Eira says dryly. "I'm officially your project now."

Neville grins. "Hey, at least you're a cool project. I mean, how many people get to say they're friends with a vampire?"

Eira shakes her head, but her lips twitch into a smile. "You're impossible."

"That's what makes me so lovable," Neville replies, winking.

As their banter continues, I find myself smiling despite everything. It's strange, seeing Eira and Neville like this—like they've known each other forever.

Maybe this is what she needs. Not just someone to help her, but someone to make her laugh, to remind her that she's still human. Or at least… mostly human.

Still, a small part of me can't help but feel left out. They're bonding, and I'm just… here. Watching. Worrying. Useless.

Eventually, the sun dips below the horizon, and the room

is bathed in a warm, golden glow. Neville stretches, his movements lazy and unhurried. "Alright, I think that's enough emotional bonding for one day. I'm starving."

Eira rolls her eyes. "You're always starving."

"And you're always cranky," Neville shoots back, grinning.

The question is out of my mouth before I can stop it. "Where's Ryker, by the way? He wasn't at the assembly."

Neville stiffens slightly, the easygoing air around him faltering for a moment. "He's… been researching since the attack," he says carefully, avoiding my gaze.

"Researching what?" I press, narrowing my eyes.

Neville shrugs, his tone casual but forced. "The rogue vampire. You know Ryker—he likes to play the hero."

His response doesn't sit well with me, but I let it go for now. Why wouldn't he tell me this himself? Why hasn't he been around?

I shake my head, standing up. "Alright. Let's get some food before Neville starts chewing on the furniture."

As we leave the room, a small sense of weirdness creeps through me. I don't know why or how but my intuition says, it is related to Ryker. I need to see him once to make sure he's okay and my mind would stop overthinking.

# 15

# Transition

The hallways of Harlow Academy stretch endlessly ahead of me, their Gothic arches and flickering sconces casting eerie shadows on the stone walls. The weight of the past few days presses down on me, heavier with each step.

Eira is back in our dorm now, curled up in her bed, quiet and withdrawn. Her silence is louder than anything she could say, a stark reminder of how much everything has changed.

But I can't let myself break. Not when the image of her pale face and those haunting puncture wounds keeps flashing through my mind. Someone here did this to her. Someone left her to deal with the aftermath of a nightmare they created.

And I have no idea who it is.

I don't realize where my feet are taking me until I find myself standing in the library. It's become my refuge, though tonight the shelves feel taller, the shadows deeper, as if the space itself is watching me.

I pull a book from the nearest shelf and sink into a corner seat. *Supernatural Myths and Realities.* The title feels mocking, a reminder of how little I know.

Flipping through the pages does nothing to quiet my thoughts. Every word blurs together, and my mind keeps returning to Eira. The girl who could light up a room with her laugh now sits in shadows, terrified of what she's becoming.

And someone here caused it.

My hand clenches around the book, my knuckles white. Whoever did this knew exactly what they were doing. This wasn't random. It wasn't a mistake. It was calculated, deliberate.

But why Eira?

Was it an attack on her, or a message meant for someone else—someone like me? The thought sends a chill down my spine, and I shove the book aside, leaning back in my chair.

The creak of a chair pulls me from my thoughts, and I glance up to see Neville settling into the seat across from me. His presence is grounding, though his serious expression makes my chest tighten further.

"You're avoiding her," he says without preamble.

I scowl, crossing my arms. "I'm not."

"You are," he counters, leaning forward. "And I get it. It's hard. But she needs you right now, Asterine. More than ever."

I look away, guilt twisting in my stomach. "I don't know what to say to her, Nev," I admit, my voice barely above a whisper.

"You don't have to say anything," he says simply. "Just be there. That's enough."

"No, it's not," I snap, frustration bubbling to the surface. "She's slipping, Neville. And I don't know how to stop it. I don't even know how to help her."

Neville's expression softens. "You're not supposed to fix her,

Asterine. That's not your job. But you can support her. That's what matters."

His words sting, though I know he's right.

"What about the person who did this to her?" I demand, my voice trembling. "Do we just let them get away with it? Do we just sit back while they ruin her life?"

Neville leans back in his chair, his gaze thoughtful. "Do you think it was someone at the Academy?"

"It has to be," I say firmly. "Who else could it be? Someone here attacked her, and they're walking around like nothing happened. Like they didn't destroy her life."

Neville nods slowly, his jaw tightening. "We'll figure it out. But don't let your anger get the better of you, Asterine. You need to stay clear-headed—for her."

I exhale sharply, leaning forward to rest my head in my hands. "It's just… I can't stop thinking about it. Every time I look at her, I see what they did, and it makes me sick."

"We'll find them," Neville says again, his tone steady. "But right now, Eira needs you more than your anger does."

The next morning, Eira insists on joining me for class. She says she feels fine, and I don't have the energy to argue. But as we walk into Calculus together, I can't shake the feeling that something's wrong.

At first, she seems normal—quiet, but present. But halfway through the lesson, I notice her shifting in her seat, her hands gripping the desk tightly.

"Eira?" I whisper, glancing at her.

She doesn't respond. Her breathing quickens, and her eyes are fixed on the boy sitting in front of us, Carson.

My stomach twists as I follow her gaze. She's staring at his neck.

"Eira," I say again, louder this time, my voice trembling.

She jerks slightly, her eyes snapping to mine. For a moment, I don't recognize her. Her pupils are dilated, and there's a wildness in her expression that makes my chest tighten.

"Asterine," she whispers, her voice strained. "I can't…"

She pushes back her chair abruptly, the screech of wood against stone drawing everyone's attention.

"Miss Ashworth, Miss Valen," Professor Lindell says sharply. "Is there a problem?"

Eira shakes her head, her movements jerky. "I—I need to go," she stammers, her voice barely audible.

Without waiting for permission, she bolts from the classroom.

I find her in the bathroom, leaning over the sink with her hands braced against the counter. Her shoulders tremble, her breath coming in short, uneven gasps.

"Eira," I say softly, stepping inside.

She doesn't look at me. Her reflection in the mirror is pale and drawn, her bloodshot eyes glassy.

"I don't know what's happening to me," she whispers, her voice trembling.

I take a step closer, my chest tightening. "You don't have to do this alone," I say firmly. "We'll figure it out. Together."

She turns to face me, tears streaming down her face. "What if I hurt someone?" she asks, her voice breaking.

"You won't," I say quickly, though I'm not sure I believe it myself.

"How can you be so sure?" she demands, her voice rising. "You don't know what it feels like, Asterine. It's like something inside me is… breaking. I don't even recognize myself anymore."

Tears prick at my eyes, but I force them back. "You're still you, Eira. And I'm not giving up on you. No matter what."

As we walk back to the dorm later that evening, my thoughts churn relentlessly.

*Who attacked her?*

It had to be someone from the Academy, someone who knew exactly what they were doing. But why? And why Eira?

My fists clench at my sides. Whoever it was, they won't get away with it.

As Eira steps into our dorm, I glance at her pale face and trembling hands. She's slipping further away, and I can feel it.

I have to find out who did this.

And when I do, they'll regret ever laying a hand on her.

# 16

# Edward Cullen Who?

The dorm is silent, but it's the kind of silence that feels loud, pressing against my ears, crawling under my skin. Beside me, Eira stirs faintly in her sleep, her face pale and hollow in the faint glow of moonlight spilling through the window.

She's been so different since the bite. Unsteady. Fragile. And yet, I feel like I'm the one unraveling.

The room feels too small tonight, the air thick and heavy, wrapping itself around my chest and refusing to let go. My heartbeat is too loud, my thoughts too sharp, and I know I won't be able to sleep.

I throw off the blanket, the chill of the room biting at my skin as I sit up. Grabbing my hoodie from the back of the chair, I pull it on, slipping out of the room as quietly as possible.

The hallway is dimly lit, the flickering sconces casting jagged shadows on the stone walls. The sharp scent of cold air greets me, but it does little to calm the whirlwind in my mind. My steps are soft, almost tentative, as I wander aimlessly through the corridors of Harlow Academy.

*Why her?*

*Who would do this?*

*What am I missing?*

The questions tumble over each other in my head, relentless and unanswered.

Me loitering around the hallways of the Harlow Academy at nights like a nocturnal animal has seem to become an everyday kind of thing. After all the incidents happening one after another without any of them giving a proper reasonable, logical answers seems to affect me like a heavy dose of caffeine and anxiety mixed together, hence the disturbed sleep cycle.

But I have to admit to myself that every time I'm out here at nights I come across disastrous revelations. I shudder at that thought.

I hope I don't come across any today.

As if I spoke to soon-

My wandering takes me deeper into the school, far past the parts of the Academy I know. The torches are sparser here, their light dim and weak, barely enough to hold back the darkness.

The air changes as I walk. It's colder, damp, and carries a faint metallic tang that makes my stomach twist. I stop at an intersection, the familiar polished stone floors giving way to something older, rougher.

To my left is the soft glow of more torches, leading back toward the main parts of the Academy. But to my right, the hallway stretches into shadows, its path barely illuminated by the occasional torch.

My instincts tell me to turn back, to take the safe, familiar route.

But something about the darker hallway pulls at me—a subtle

hum, a faint vibration in the air that I can't quite explain.

I take a deep breath, steeling myself, and step into the shadows.

The farther I go, the stranger it feels. The air grows heavier, almost oppressive, as though the weight of the building itself is pressing down on me.

The walls here are different, rougher and uneven, with cracks that spiderweb through the stone. Ancient tapestries hang limp and forgotten, their once-vivid colors faded to dull, dusty remnants. The designs are grotesque—figures twisted into impossible shapes, eyes that seem to follow me as I move.

Cobwebs drape the corners, their delicate threads shimmering faintly in the dim torchlight. Dust coats the floor in thick layers, my footsteps leaving a trail behind me.

*No one comes here.*

The realization sends a chill down my spine. This part of the school has been abandoned for years, maybe decades. But why?

I almost miss it. At the end of the hallway, tucked into a corner and partially hidden behind a tattered tapestry, is a door.

It's small and unassuming, its dark wood warped with age. The handle is rusted, flecks of red-brown flaking off as I reach out to touch it. My fingers hesitate, hovering over the tarnished metal as unease prickles at the back of my neck.

The tapestry hanging over it is barely intact, its fabric torn and frayed. The design catches my eye—something about it feels wrong. It shows a forest of twisted trees, their branches clawing at the sky, with shadowy figures standing among them. The figures seem almost alive, shifting and flickering in the dim light.

I pull the tapestry aside, revealing the door fully.

A strange symbol is carved into the wood—spiraling lines that twist and overlap, creating a design that almost seems to move. My stomach churns as I stare at it, a faint nausea curling in my gut.

The air hums faintly, vibrating just beneath the surface.

*Don't open it.*

The thought whispers in the back of my mind, but curiosity burns hotter than fear. My hand wraps around the handle, and I push the door open.

The door creaks loudly, the sound echoing through the empty hallway.

Beyond it is a staircase, narrow and spiraling downward into complete darkness. The light from the hallway barely reaches the first few steps, swallowed quickly by the shadows below.

I take a step forward, the cold air rushing up to greet me. The metallic tang in the air is stronger now, mingling with the earthy scent of damp stone.

Each step feels heavier than the last, the creak of the wood beneath my feet unnaturally loud. The deeper I go, the more the air vibrates, a low hum that seems to resonate in my bones.

When I reach the bottom, the staircase opens into a narrow tunnel, its walls lined with faintly glowing runes.

The glow of the runes is faint, just enough to see by, their soft blue light casting eerie shadows on the uneven stone walls. The symbols are intricate and precise, their lines flowing like water.

The hum is louder here, almost deafening in its intensity. It's not a sound—it's a sensation, a vibration that buzzes beneath my skin and makes my head feel too full.

I move cautiously, each step slow and deliberate. The tunnel seems to stretch endlessly, twisting and turning in ways that make no sense.

The carvings on the walls grow more complex the farther I go. At first, they're just runes, but soon they evolve into shapes and figures—faces with hollow eyes, mouths open in silent screams.

I don't know how long I've been walking when I hear it—a faint rustling ahead, followed by a quiet thud.

My breath catches, my pulse quickening as I press myself against the wall. The shadows ahead seem thicker, almost alive, shifting and writhing in the dim light.

And then I see it.

A figure stands at the far end of the tunnel, their back to me. They're hunched over, their movements slow and deliberate.

I take a step closer, my footsteps silent against the stone. The metallic scent is overwhelming now, thick and cloying, and my stomach churns as I realize what it is.

Blood.

The figure holds a bag in their hands, the dark liquid gleaming faintly in the runes' light.

I take another step, the faint sound of my foot scuffing against the ground breaking the silence.

The figure freezes.

Slowly, they turn, and the glow of the runes illuminates their face.

My breath catches, my chest tightening as I stare into the midnight black eyes and copper hair of Ryker.

Ryker's lips are stained crimson, the faint trace of blood catching the light as he stares at me.

"Asterine?" he says, his voice low, almost hesitant.

I can't move. My mind races, the image of him burned into

my vision.

Blood on his mouth. Blood on his hands.

And no explanation.

# 17

## Lies, they just never stop

The air in the tunnel feels thick and suffocating as I stare at Ryker. His midnight-black eyes lock onto mine, their usual teasing warmth replaced by something darker, something unfamiliar. The faint glow of the runes etched into the walls casts flickering shadows over his copper hair, which is tousled and slightly damp. But it's his lips that hold my attention, and not in the way they usually do—they're stained with blood, gleaming faintly in the dim light.

I can't move. My legs feel rooted to the ground, my chest tightening with each shallow breath. A knot of disbelief, anger, and something I can't yet name coils in my stomach.

"Asterine," he says softly, his voice low and careful, like he's trying not to spook a cornered animal.

I stumble back, my feet scraping against the rough stone floor. My heart hammers against my ribs, each beat loud and deafening.

"Stay away from me," I whisper, barely able to get the words out. My voice trembles, almost swallowed by the hum of the air around us.

Ryker raises his hands slowly, his movements deliberate, as though he's trying to reassure me. "It's not what it looks like."

A sharp, humorless laugh bursts out of me, high-pitched and shaky. "Not what it looks like?" My voice rises, trembling with fear and rage. "Then what exactly is it, Ryker? Because it looks like—"

"A vampire," he says quietly, cutting me off.

The word hangs in the air between us, heavy and irreversible.

I stare at him, my mind spinning. My throat tightens as I try to form words, but everything feels unreal, foreign, impossible. "You're a vampire?"

"Yes," he admits, his tone steady but raw, edged with something I don't want to name. "I wanted to tell you, but—"

"But what?" I snap, my voice cracking. "You thought I wouldn't notice? That you could keep it hidden forever? How long were you planning to lie to me, Ryker?"

"I wasn't lying," he says firmly, taking a cautious step toward me. "I just—"

"Don't!" I flinch, stepping back, and he stops in his tracks. My voice shakes as I whisper, "Don't come any closer."

He freezes, his jaw tightening, his hands lowering slightly. His expression flickers—frustration, regret, and something that almost looks like guilt.

"Asterine, please," he says, his voice softer now. "You have to understand—"

"Understand what?" I interrupt, my eyes stinging with unshed tears. "That everything I thought I knew about you was a lie? That you've been hiding this part of yourself while pretending to be someone you're not?"

"It's not like that," he insists, his tone almost pleading. "I didn't tell you because I didn't want you to look at me like this."

"Like what?" I demand, my voice breaking. "Like I don't even know who you are?"

The words echo in the tunnel, sharp and cutting, leaving a heavy silence in their wake.

"I didn't hurt Eira," he says quietly, his dark eyes searching mine. "You have to believe me. I would never hurt her. I would never hurt you."

His words slice through me, and for a fleeting moment, I want to believe him. But the image of his bloodstained lips flashes in my mind, and the doubt crushes any flicker of trust.

"I… I can't do this," I whisper, my voice trembling. "I can't look at you right now."

"Asterine, wait," he starts, stepping forward again, but I don't let him finish.

I turn and run.

The cold air of the hallway hits me like a slap as I burst out of the tunnel. My breath comes in short, shallow gasps, and my legs burn with the effort of running. My chest tightens, but I push forward, the need to escape overwhelming everything else.

When I reach the door to my dorm, my hands tremble as I fumble with the handle. The second it clicks open, I stumble inside and slam it shut behind me.

The room is dark, quiet except for the soft sound of Eira's breathing. She's curled up on her side in her bed, her face peaceful under the faint glow of moonlight spilling through the window.

I press my back against the door, sliding down until I'm sitting on the cold floor. My chest heaves, my head spinning as I try to steady my breathing.

What just happened?

The image of Ryker's face, his dark, unreadable eyes, and the blood on his lips flares in my mind, sending a fresh wave of panic crashing over me. My hands clench into fists, my nails digging into my palms as I fight to keep control.

But it's no use.

The tears come suddenly, hot and blinding, spilling over as a sob wrenches itself from my throat.

I bury my face in my hands, my shoulders shaking. You trusted him. You thought he was different. And now…

My sobs grow louder, my breath hitching painfully. What else has he been lying about? How long has he been hiding this? What if he hurt Eira?

The thought twists my stomach, leaving me nauseated. I don't want to believe it. I don't want to think he could do something so terrible. But the blood on his mouth, the bag in his hand—it feels too damning.

My heart aches, a sharp mix of anger, betrayal, and fear.

I press my fists against my temples, rocking slightly as the panic claws at my chest. My breath comes in shallow gasps, each one more painful than the last.

"Stop," I whisper to myself, my voice shaking. "Just stop."

But the thoughts won't stop. They swirl around me, relentless and suffocating.

I don't know how long I sit there, my back against the door, my knees pulled to my chest. My sobs have subsided into quiet sniffles, and my breathing is slowly evening out, though my chest still feels tight.

Eira shifts in her sleep, murmuring something incoherent before falling silent again.

I glance at her, my heart twisting. She doesn't know. She

didn't see. And yet, she's the one paying the price for all of this.

Dragging myself to my feet, I wipe at my face with the sleeve of my hoodie. My legs feel weak, my body heavy as I stumble toward my bed and sink onto the edge.

The questions buzz in my mind, quieter now but no less persistent. How long has he been lying? How many secrets has he kept?

I think of his face as he tried to explain, the regret in his eyes, the softness in his voice.

And for a moment, I almost believe him.

But the blood—the undeniable proof of what he is—shatters that belief before it can take hold.

I lie down, staring at the ceiling, the weight of the night pressing down on me like a physical force.

I can't deal with Ryker right now. Whatever he is, whatever he's done, it's too much. Too complicated.

For now, my focus has to be on Eira. She needs me more than I need answers about Ryker.

But someday, I'll get those answers.

And when I do, I won't let anyone's lies blind me again.

# 18

# Hysteria

The days since that night have been a blur, each one passing like the last, wrapped in the same unbearable weight of confusion and distrust. I haven't seen Ryker since I fled the tunnel, and I'm not sure I even want to. His face, bloodied and conflicted, is burned into my memory, every time I close my eyes, every time I take a breath. The image twists my insides in ways I can't explain, a strange mix of anger, betrayal, and a lingering, hollow emptiness.

I'm trying—desperately—to push it all aside. But I can't. It's there, right under the surface, just waiting for the smallest crack to let it all spill out again.

So I keep busy. I bury myself in distractions, trying not to think about the mess I'm in. My schoolwork, my friends, everything is just one big blur. But no matter how much I focus on what's in front of me, my thoughts keep drifting back to Ryker.

His words. His confession.

*I didn't want you to find out like this.*

It wasn't just a lie. It was a betrayal.

The last few days have been just as hard on Eira. She's getting worse. It's subtle at first—little things, like the way her eyes seem to linger a little too long on the pulse in someone's neck or the way she flinches every time someone gets too close. But the cracks are starting to show, and no amount of reassurance can mask the fact that she's slipping into something she doesn't want to be.

I can see it in her eyes. She's scared. Terrified. And so am I.

I try to comfort her, try to be the friend I know I should be, but it's becoming harder. The words feel empty, and the solutions I suggest sound hollow even to me. She's fighting an enemy inside herself that I don't understand, and I have no idea how to help her fight it.

She's withdrawn even further now, retreating into herself. The sparkle in her eyes has dimmed, replaced with a distant, haunted look that makes my chest ache.

"Eira," I say one evening as we sit in the common room, a textbook open between us, though neither of us is really paying attention. "Are you okay?"

Her gaze flickers toward me for a brief moment, but she doesn't answer. She just nods, a forced smile pulling at her lips.

"I'm fine, Asterine," she mutters, but I can see the lie in her eyes.

I want to push her for more. I want to demand the truth, to make her tell me what's going on inside her, but I can't. Not when I'm still trying to figure out my own mess.

So instead, I sit there, in silence, watching as she slowly fades away, piece by piece.

The school, as always, seems to hum with the quiet knowledge of its secrets. The walls, the halls, the ancient bookshelves stacked with centuries of knowledge—it all feels so suffocating. Every day I pass the same hallways, the same classrooms, the same students, and every day, it feels like the walls are closing in a little more.

I spend my time in the library, pouring over ancient texts, hoping for a glimpse of something—anything—that can help me understand what's happening to Eira. But the more I read, the more questions pile up, and the fewer answers I seem to find. There are stories of blood curses, of magic that binds people to unnatural forces, but none of it seems to explain what Eira is going through.

I sift through pages of lore and spells, trying to find something that fits. A cure, an antidote, a way to stop the hunger gnawing at her from the inside. But the deeper I go, the more I wonder if I'm looking for answers in the wrong places.

*There's got to be something.*

Frustration builds in my chest as I turn another page, my fingers trembling with the weight of it all. I feel like I'm drowning in unanswered questions, each page more confusing than the last.

"Hey," Neville's voice cuts through my thoughts, pulling me from the depths of the book. "You've been at this for hours."

I glance up at him, his face drawn with concern. "I have to find something, Nev," I mutter, pushing my hair back from my face. "I have to help her."

"You will," he says softly, sitting down across from me. "But you can't do it alone."

I look at him, my heart aching at the sight of my brother— always the stable one, the one who keeps his cool when everything around him falls apart.

"I just don't know what to do," I whisper, the weight of my

emotions making my voice crack.

He doesn't say anything at first, just looks at me like he's trying to decide whether or not to press me further. But then he leans forward, his voice low. "You need to tell me what's going on, Asterine. About… everything."

I shake my head, my thoughts tumbling over each other. How do I explain to him what's happening without sounding insane? How do I tell him about Ryker, about the vampire, and about how my world feels like it's crumbling beneath me?

"I can't," I say, my voice breaking. "Not yet."

Neville sighs, his frustration palpable, but he doesn't push me further. Instead, he simply leans back in his chair, looking out the window. I can see the worry etched into his features, but he doesn't question me again.

I try to push Ryker out of my thoughts, but it's impossible. Every moment I spend avoiding him, I wonder if I'm doing the right thing. Should I face him? Should I hear him out? Or is it better to keep my distance until I'm sure of what's going on?

I don't know.

All I know is that seeing him that night, his lips stained with blood, made something inside me snap. I can't look at him right now. I can't hear his voice or see his face without remembering the way he looked when he was lying to me.

So I avoid him. I skip classes when I know he'll be there. I take alternate routes, walk faster when I see him coming. It's childish, but it's the only way I know to protect myself from whatever it is that I'm feeling.

I think about confronting him, about getting the answers I so desperately need, but I'm not ready. Not yet.

Neville has been watching me. I can tell. He doesn't ask

questions, but he's been there, sitting beside me when I'm reading, waiting until I finally look up and meet his gaze.

"Asterine," he says one evening, his voice laced with concern. "What's going on with you? You haven't been yourself lately."

I swallow hard, my heart pounding in my chest. "I'm fine," I lie. "Just tired."

But Neville doesn't look convinced. "You're avoiding everyone. You're not sleeping. You can't keep doing this alone."

I want to tell him the truth—everything that's been weighing on me, everything that's broken inside me. But I can't. Not yet.

"I'm fine, Neville. I just need some time."

He doesn't argue. Instead, he sits there, his eyes filled with understanding that I don't feel I deserve.

That night, when the weight of the day becomes too much to bear, I let myself break.

I'm sitting by the window again, my eyes dry from the tears I've been holding in all day. The moonlight spills across the floor, casting long shadows that seem to stretch endlessly toward me. I close my eyes, my chest tight, and the tears finally come.

They're quiet at first, just a trickle, but soon they're flooding over me, a torrent of everything I've been holding in for so long. The confusion. The fear. The frustration. The betrayal.

I let it all out, sobbing into the sleeve of my hoodie, my body wracked with the weight of it all. The vulnerability of it stings, but it's the only release I have left.

I wish I could tell someone. I wish I could just scream, let all of it go. But I can't. Not yet.

And for the first time in days, I let myself feel the full extent of the loss—of Eira slipping further away from me, of the lies surrounding me, of the fear I can't shake.

# 19

# A very Vampy-friendship

The silence between Eira and me was heavy, broken only by the faint shuffle of her hesitant steps. The hallway stretched before us, dimly lit by flickering sconces that cast long shadows on the stone walls. It felt like the building itself was holding its breath, waiting to see what would happen next.

"I don't think I can do this, Asterine," Eira whispered, her voice trembling.

I stopped, turning to face her. Her shoulders were hunched, her normally vibrant face pale and drawn. She wasn't looking at me—her gaze was fixed on the floor, her hands clutching the edges of her sleeves like they might anchor her to reality.

"You can," I said softly, though my heart twisted at the fear in her eyes. "I'll be with you the whole time."

She glanced up, her eyes shimmering with unshed tears. "But what if I can't stop?"

Her words hit me like a punch to the gut. I didn't have an answer for her. I didn't know if this would help, if it would make things better or worse. But I couldn't let her spiral into that fear. I had to be strong, for her.

"We'll deal with that if it happens," I said firmly, placing a hand on her arm. "But you're not going to lose yourself, Eira. You're stronger than this."

She nodded hesitantly, though the fear didn't leave her eyes.

The medical wing was colder than the rest of the Academy, the sterile smell of antiseptic mingling with something faintly metallic. A nurse greeted us at the entrance, her expression kind but professional.

"Eira Valen?"

Eira froze at the sound of her name, and I could see her hands shaking. I stepped closer to her, giving her arm a reassuring squeeze.

"That's me," Eira said, though her voice was barely above a whisper.

"Come with me," the nurse said gently.

We followed her down a quiet corridor and into a small, private room. It was simple—just a cushioned chair, a side table, and a tray holding a single blood bag. The sight of it made my stomach churn, but I forced myself to stay composed.

Eira, on the other hand, went rigid. She stared at the bag like it might attack her.

"I don't want to do this," she said, her voice breaking.

I stepped in front of her, placing my hands on her shoulders. "Eira, listen to me," I said firmly. "This is just to help you. It's not about changing who you are. It's about giving you control. You need this."

Her breathing was shallow, her eyes darting between me and the blood bag. For a moment, I thought she might run.

The nurse stepped forward, her voice calm and steady. "This is part of the adjustment process. The first feeding is always the hardest, but it's necessary to stabilize your system and ease the hunger. You're safe here."

Eira hesitated, then nodded slowly. She moved to the chair, her steps unsteady, and sat down like her legs might give out at any moment.

The nurse handed her the blood bag, and Eira took it with trembling hands. She stared at it, her chest rising and falling rapidly.

"It's okay," I said, crouching beside her. "You've got this."

She looked at me, her lip trembling, then brought the bag to her lips. Her first sip was tentative, almost reluctant, but the moment the blood touched her tongue, something changed.

Her eyes widened, her breathing slowed, and she drank deeply. The transformation was both subtle and unnerving— the tension in her shoulders eased, but there was something almost primal in the way she held the bag, her fingers gripping it tightly.

I stayed by her side the whole time, my heart aching as I watched my best friend succumb to something she never asked for.

When she finished, she set the empty bag on the tray, her hands still shaking. "I hate this," she whispered, tears streaming down her face.

I reached for her hand, squeezing it tightly. "I know," I said softly. "But you're still you, Eira. This doesn't change that."

She looked at me, her eyes searching mine. "What if it does?"

"It won't," I said, my voice firm. "We won't let it."

Later that evening, Eira was curled up on her bed, a blanket draped over her shoulders like a protective shield. Neville sat on the edge of my bed, his arms crossed as we discussed the Academy's plan for Eira.

"So, they're just going to provide her with blood bags on a schedule?" Neville asked, his brow furrowed.

"That's the plan," I said, glancing at Eira. She hadn't said much since we got back, her eyes distant as she stared at the floor.

"And this is supposed to help her control everything?" Neville pressed.

"That's what they said," I replied, my voice tinged with frustration. "They said it'll stabilize her hunger and help with the mood swings and... everything else."

Neville nodded slowly, but his expression remained skeptical. "And how do you feel about it?" he asked, directing the question to Eira.

She shrugged, her voice small. "I hate it," she admitted. "But I don't want to hurt anyone. I don't have a choice."

"You're doing the right thing," I said quickly, my tone firm. "This is about keeping you safe—and everyone else too."

Eira gave me a weak smile, though it didn't reach her eyes. "Thanks, Asterine."

A sharp knock at the door jolted me from my thoughts, the sound slicing through the tense quiet of the room. My stomach twisted as Neville stood to answer it, his movements casual—unaware of how that simple sound had already unraveled me.

*Please don't let it be him.*

But when Neville opened the door, my worst fear stood on the other side.

Ryker.

He looked almost the same as he always did—copper hair tousled just enough to seem effortless, his dark eyes sharp and piercing. But tonight, there was something different about him, something heavier in the way he carried himself. He scanned the room quickly, his gaze stopping the moment it landed on me.

"Asterine," he said softly, his voice low and careful, like he was approaching a wounded animal.

I stiffened. My hands clenched into fists at my sides, my jaw tightening as his presence filled the room. The memory of the tunnel came rushing back with brutal clarity—his bloodstained lips, the bag in his hands, and the way my trust in him had shattered in an instant.

I couldn't breathe.

I wanted to yell at him, to tell him to leave, but the words caught in my throat. My chest tightened as a wave of anger and something else—something I didn't want to name—crashed over me.

Neville frowned, glancing between us. "What's going on here?" he asked, his voice edged with suspicion.

Neither of us answered.

"Okay," Neville said, crossing his arms. "Someone better start talking. What the hell is going on?"

Ryker sighed, running a hand through his hair. "She found out," he said quietly, his eyes flickering toward me again.

"Found out what?" Neville asked, his tone sharper now.

"That I'm a vampire," Ryker admitted.

The room fell into a stunned silence, the weight of his words hanging in the air like a storm cloud.

Neville turned to me, his eyes wide with shock. "Asterine, you—"

"I saw him," I said, my voice brittle, cutting him off. "In the tunnel. With blood on his mouth and a bag in his hand."

I could feel the blood rushing to my face, the mixture of anger and humiliation burning beneath my skin. Saying the words out loud made it feel real all over again, and I hated it.

Neville's face twisted with fury as he turned back to Ryker. "You idiot!" he snapped. "How could you be so careless? Do you even realize what you've done?"

Ryker didn't flinch under Neville's anger. Instead, he stood tall, his expression calm but tense. "I didn't mean for her to find out like that," he said.

"Well, she did!" Neville shouted, his voice rising. "And now look at this mess!"

Ryker's calm exterior cracked for a moment, frustration flashing in his eyes. "I didn't hurt her," he said firmly, his voice steady despite the tension in the room. "And I didn't hurt Eira. You have to believe me."

I folded my arms, my heart pounding so loudly I could hear it in my ears. "Why should I?" I snapped, my voice trembling. "You've been lying to me this entire time."

His gaze softened as he looked at me, and for a split second, I thought I saw regret in his eyes. "I didn't lie," he said quietly. "I just didn't tell you."

"Same thing," I shot back.

Neville let out a heavy sigh, rubbing his temples as if trying to ward off a headache. "Because I told him not to," he muttered.

I froze, staring at him. "What?"

Neville avoided my gaze, his expression pinched with guilt. "I told him not to tell you," he admitted, his voice quieter now. "I thought it would be better if you didn't know."

"You thought it would be better?" I repeated, my voice rising as anger bubbled to the surface. "Neville, you lied to me too?"

"I was trying to protect you," he said, his tone defensive.

"By keeping me in the dark?" I snapped. "You don't get to decide what I can or can't handle, Neville!"

My chest felt like it was about to burst, the betrayal cutting deeper than I wanted to admit. My brother—the one person I thought I could always rely on—had been part of this lie.

Ryker stepped forward, his expression serious. "Asterine," he said, his voice soft but insistent. "I didn't tell you because Neville thought it was the right thing to do. But I swear, I didn't hurt Eira. I would never hurt her—or you."

My throat tightened, and for a moment, I couldn't speak. The sincerity in his voice, the way his eyes pleaded with me, made it hard to hold onto the anger that had been burning inside me.

But then I remembered the tunnel—the blood, the betrayal— and the anger surged back, stronger than before.

*Why does he sound so convincing?*

*Why do I still feel like I can trust him, even after everything?*

The questions churned in my mind, each one twisting the knife deeper. I hated how conflicted I felt, how part of me still wanted to believe him despite the evidence in front of me.

But more than that, I hated how Neville had kept this from me. My own brother—my twin—had decided I wasn't strong enough to handle the truth.

"You both lied to me," I said finally, my voice shaking. "Do you have any idea how that feels?"

Neville opened his mouth to respond, but I cut him off. "No. Don't. I don't want to hear your excuses. You don't get to decide what I can or can't handle, Neville. That's not your choice."

"Wait," Eira said suddenly, her voice breaking through the tension. "You're a vampire?"

Ryker turned to her, nodding slowly. "Yes."

Eira stared at him for a moment, her face a mix of shock and something else—relief. "Then… you can help me. Can't you?"

Ryker hesitated, his eyes flickering to me before settling on Eira. "I can," he said finally. "I'll teach you how to manage everything—how to control it. You don't have to go through this alone."

Eira's shoulders sagged, a small, shaky smile breaking through her otherwise tense expression. "Thank you," she whispered.

I watched the exchange in silence, my emotions a tangled mess.

*How can she trust him so easily?*

*How can she not feel the same betrayal I do?*

As the room fell into an uneasy quiet, I felt the weight of everything pressing down on me—the lies, the secrets, the betrayals.

I needed space. I needed time to think.

But for now, all I could do was sit in the aftermath of the truth, trying to figure out where to go from here.

# 20

# Bridging Gaps

The dorm felt unusually quiet this evening. Eira was sitting cross-legged on her bed, her back against the headboard, while I sat at my desk, absentmindedly flipping through a notebook I wasn't actually reading. The light from the desk lamp cast a warm glow over the room, but it did little to chase away the weight hanging in the air.

"How are you feeling?" I asked, breaking the silence.

Eira looked up, a small, tired smile pulling at her lips. "Better, I think. Less… tense."

I nodded, but the worry didn't leave me. "That's good. It's a start, right?"

She shrugged, her fingers fidgeting with the hem of her sweater. "I guess. But it's still so weird, Asterine. All of it. I mean, I don't even know how I'm supposed to go back to my family like this."

The vulnerability in her voice cut through me. I turned in my chair to face her, leaning forward slightly. "What do you mean?"

Eira's eyes dropped to her lap, her voice barely above a

whisper. "How do I look my parents in the eye and pretend everything's fine when I'm… this? When I have to drink blood just to stay sane?"

"Eira…"

She shook her head, her voice growing more strained. "What if they find out? What if they hate me for it? I don't even know how I'm supposed to act normal around them anymore."

I got up and moved to sit beside her on the bed, placing a hand on her arm. "Hey, listen to me," I said gently. "Your family loves you. They're not going to hate you for something you couldn't control."

She gave a shaky laugh, but there was no humor in it. "You don't know that. I don't even know that."

Her words made my chest ache. I couldn't imagine how terrifying it must be for her, knowing her entire life had been upended in a way she couldn't explain to the people she cared about the most.

"You don't have to figure it all out right now," I said softly. "One step at a time, okay? You've already come so far."

Eira glanced at me, her eyes shimmering with unshed tears. "Do you really think so?"

"I know so," I said firmly.

The tension in her expression softened, and for the first time in days, I saw a flicker of the old Eira—the bright, determined girl who wasn't afraid to face whatever came her way.

"Ryker helped a lot today," she said after a moment, her voice quieter now.

My stomach tightened at the mention of his name, but I forced myself to keep my expression neutral. "Yeah?"

She nodded. "He's… different when it's just the two of us. He's patient, calm. He didn't make me feel stupid for not knowing anything. And he explained everything—what to expect, how to handle it, even how to manage the cravings."

A part of me wanted to snap at her, to remind her that Ryker wasn't exactly the shining example of honesty and transparency. But the relief in her voice stopped me.

"I'm glad he's helping," I said instead, though the words felt stiff on my tongue.

Eira gave me a sidelong glance, a small smirk tugging at her lips. "You don't have to sound so enthusiastic about it."

I rolled my eyes, but my cheeks burned. "I'm still mad at him," I admitted.

She tilted her head. "I know. And you have every right to be. But... maybe cut him some slack? At least a little?"

I raised an eyebrow, my defenses immediately going up. "Cut him some slack?"

Eira nodded, her expression thoughtful. "Yeah. I mean, he didn't tell you because Neville told him not to, right? And from what he said today, he's been carrying that guilt around for a while."

Her words stung more than I wanted to admit. I crossed my arms, staring at the floor. "It's not just about him not telling me. It's... everything. The lies, the secrets, the way everyone seems to think I can't handle the truth."

"I get that," Eira said softly. "But you're putting all that anger on Ryker when maybe some of it should be aimed at Neville."

My stomach churned at her words, but I couldn't deny the truth in them. Neville had lied to me too, had kept me in the dark when I deserved to know what was going on. But the thought of being mad at him felt wrong. He was my brother, the one person I'd always thought I could rely on.

Eira placed a hand on my arm, her touch grounding me. "I'm

not saying Ryker doesn't deserve some of your anger," she said. "But maybe… just maybe… he's not the villain you want him to be."

After Eira went to bed, I sat by the window, staring out at the Academy grounds. The moonlight bathed the gardens in a pale, ghostly glow, the shadows stretching like fingers across the stone pathways.

Eira's words echoed in my mind, refusing to be ignored.

*Maybe some of it should be aimed at Neville.*

I hated how much that made sense. Neville had been hiding things from me for weeks—maybe longer. And for what? To protect me? To keep me from falling apart?

The thought made my chest tighten with a mix of anger and hurt. I wasn't some fragile thing that needed to be shielded from the truth. I could handle it—at least, I wanted to believe I could.

And then there was Ryker.

The memory of him standing in my doorway, his expression heavy with regret, played over and over in my mind. He hadn't tried to justify himself or make excuses. He'd just… been honest.

*He didn't tell you because Neville told him not to.*

It didn't erase the betrayal I felt, but it complicated it. I couldn't ignore the fact that he'd been put in an impossible position, stuck between what Neville thought was best and what he might have wanted to do himself.

I thought about Eira and how much better she seemed after her session with Ryker. She'd looked calmer, more in control— like she was finally starting to find her footing.

Maybe Eira was right. Maybe Ryker wasn't the villain in this story.

But if he wasn't, then who was?

My thoughts drifted to my parents, to the way they'd sent me here without a second thought. What had they known? What had they kept from me?

*Why does everyone in my life think they need to protect me from the truth?*

The thought made my stomach twist, my fists clenching in my lap. I hated feeling like I was the last to know, like I was always one step behind everyone else.

But not anymore.

I didn't know how, but I was going to get to the bottom of this. About Eira, about Ryker, about everything.

The next morning, Eira was already up when I woke, sitting at her desk with a notebook open in front of her. She looked more focused, more present than she had in days.

"Morning," I said, rubbing the sleep from my eyes.

"Morning," she replied, glancing at me with a small smile.

I watched her for a moment, noting the way her shoulders weren't as hunched, the way her hands weren't trembling like they had been before. She seemed... better.

"How are you feeling?" I asked.

"Okay," she said, her smile widening slightly. "Better than I have in a while."

I nodded, a small sense of relief settling in my chest. "That's good. You seem... more like yourself."

Eira shrugged, but I could see the pride in her eyes. "Ryker helped a lot. He showed me some breathing techniques to keep the cravings in check, and he explained what to expect as things change. It's still hard, but... it's manageable."

Her words tugged at something deep inside me—something I wasn't ready to face.

"That's great, Eira," I said, forcing a smile.

She nodded, her gaze thoughtful. "It is. But you know… I think you should talk to him. I know you're mad, and you have every right to be, but… he's not the bad guy, Asterine."

I sighed, running a hand through my hair. "I'll think about it."

Eira gave me a knowing look but didn't push further.

As the day went on, Eira's words lingered in my mind, weaving themselves into my thoughts until they were impossible to ignore.

Neville. Ryker. My parents.

Each one of them had kept something from me, had decided I didn't deserve to know the truth. And now, I was left trying to piece it all together, to figure out where I stood in a web of lies and secrets.

But one thing was clear: I wasn't going to let them keep me in the dark anymore.

I didn't know how, but I was going to find the answers.

No more lies. No more secrets.

# 21

# Heightened senses

The dorm is disconcertingly quiet, the kind of stillness that amplifies every creak, every rustle, and every fleeting thought. Eira is sitting at her desk, flipping through a textbook, but it's clear she's not really reading it. Her face is illuminated by the soft, golden glow of the desk lamp, but her eyes are distant, lost in thought.

I sit on my bed, notebook open in front of me, pretending to write notes for an assignment. But my mind isn't on schoolwork. It drifts aimlessly, tangled up in a maze of questions I don't know how to ask and don't know how to answer.

Eira sighs, her breath heavy in the otherwise still room. I glance at her, watching as she runs her fingers over the pages, but her focus is nowhere to be found.

"How are you feeling?" I ask, breaking the silence that has settled between us.

She looks up, her gaze meeting mine. There's something guarded in her expression—vulnerable, yet resolute. "Better," she says simply, her voice steady. "Stronger."

I nod slowly, though the answer doesn't satisfy the gnawing curiosity that's been building inside me. "Eira, can I ask you something?"

She gives me a confused look but nods. "Of course. What's up?"

I hesitate, unsure how to phrase the question that's been on my mind for days. "What's it… like? Being a vampire?"

Her face softens as she leans back in her chair, the usual playfulness in her eyes dimming a little. "It's weird," she admits, her tone quieter now. "Like I'm the same person, but also… not. Everything feels sharper. I can hear things that weren't there before, smell things from across the room. It's like the world is louder, brighter, and more intense."

I frown, imagining how that must feel. "Does it… hurt?"

"No," she replies, shaking her head. "It's just overwhelming sometimes. But Ryker's been helping me control it. He's been showing me how to deal with it, how to use it without losing myself."

I catch myself leaning forward, hanging on her every word. "What else has he taught you?"

She shrugs, though I can see her excitement bubbling underneath. "The basics. How to deal with the hunger, how to use my senses. He said we'll get into more advanced stuff in the next session."

"Advanced stuff?" I echo, my mind already racing with possibilities. "Like what?"

Eira smiles faintly, her eyes twinkling with a mix of curiosity and nervousness. "I don't know. He didn't say. But he said we'd try new things."

Hours pass, and the room remains thick with unspoken words, the quiet stretching between us like a bridge neither of us knows how to cross. Eira is still quiet, occasionally jotting down something in her notebook but always seeming distant. I can feel the unease creeping in, but I don't know how to reach her, how to help her find her footing in this new life.

Finally, she turns to me, her voice hesitant, pulling me out of my spiral. "Hey, Asterine?"

I look up, blinking. "Yeah?"

"So… Ryker's got a night session planned for me," she says casually, but there's something in her tone that makes me pause.

I raise an eyebrow. "And?"

She hesitates for a moment, clearly gathering her thoughts. "And… I was wondering if you'd come with me."

I blink, thrown off by the sudden request. "Why?"

Eira fidgets with her sleeve, avoiding my gaze. "Because it's late, and it might get awkward. And, well, I'd rather have someone there with me. You know, just to cheer me on."

I stare at her for a moment, trying to gauge whether she's serious or just trying to deflect. "Cheer you on?"

"Yes," she says, her voice taking on a mock serious tone. "It's important to have an audience for these things. Especially if I'm about to embarrass myself."

I let out a long breath, feeling a bit of the tension in me ease. "Eira, I'm not sure—"

"Please?" she interrupts, her voice soft, vulnerable. "I don't want to go alone."

I feel my resolve falter at the sound of her voice—so small, so uncertain. It's like she's asking for reassurance, and I can't ignore that.

"Fine," I mutter, rolling my eyes. "But you owe me."

Eira's face lights up with relief, and a genuine smile stretches across her face. "Thanks, Asterine! You won't regret it, I promise."

The November air is biting as we step outside, and I pull my jacket tighter around me. The cold feels sharper now that the sun has long set, the moon hanging high in the sky like a silent witness to everything unfolding.

Ryker is waiting for us near the gates, his figure framed by the pale moonlight. He's leaning against a post, his arms crossed as he watches us approach.

I can't help but notice how natural he looks in the dim light, how effortlessly he blends into the shadows. His copper hair catches the moonlight, almost glowing against the dark sky. His eyes, dark as night, meet mine as we approach, and for a split second, I feel the weight of his gaze settle on me. It's unsettling—like he can see through all of me.

"Ladies," he greets us, his tone smooth and calm.

I don't respond, but I can feel my body stiffen as we walk past him. The air between us feels thick, a heavy current I can't escape.

We follow him through the gates and into the forest, the trees looming like silent sentinels in the dark. The scent of earth and pine fills the air, clean and sharp. The crunch of leaves beneath our boots is the only sound, and it's oddly soothing, grounding me in the moment.

As we walk, I can't help but steal glances at Ryker. He moves with a fluidity that's almost predatory, his movements deliberate but effortless, like he's a part of the night itself.

*What is he? What else is he hiding?* I can feel the question gnawing at me, even as I try to ignore it.

After what feels like an eternity, we reach a clearing surrounded by towering oaks. The moonlight bathes the space in an ethereal glow, the trees casting long shadows that stretch like fingers toward the earth.

"This is far enough," Ryker says, his voice breaking through the silence. "The headmaster gave me permission to bring you here, but we need to be quick."

Eira nods eagerly, her face alight with excitement. I, however, remain where I am, my arms crossed as the cold seeps deeper into my skin.

# 22

# Abilities

Ryker steps into the center of the clearing, his posture confident as he looks between us. "You've seen some of what vampires can do," he begins, his voice steady. "But there's much more to it than just speed and strength."

Eira leans forward, her interest piqued. I stay back, watching closely but unable to suppress the growing discomfort in my chest.

"First," Ryker continues, "our physical abilities—speed, strength, heightened senses. But it doesn't stop there. We're immortal—unless killed by an oak-wood stake to the heart. And then there's mind persuasion, which allows us to influence the thoughts or actions of others."

I freeze at the mention of mind persuasion. "You can control people's minds?" My voice trembles, but I can't stop the words from escaping.

Ryker looks at me, his expression unreadable. "To an extent," he admits. "It doesn't work on everyone, and it's not foolproof. But yes, it's one of our abilities."

I swallow hard, trying to steady my breath. The thought

of someone manipulating my mind, twisting my thoughts without me knowing, makes my stomach twist.

Ryker glances at Eira. "Let me show you."

Before either of us can react, Ryker's body shifts, and in the blink of an eye, he's gone—nothing but a blur of movement.

Eira gasps, her hands flying to her mouth in surprise. I blink, trying to follow his movement, but he's already back, standing by a tree on the opposite side of the clearing.

"That's... amazing," Eira says, her voice full of awe.

Ryker grins. "That's just the beginning."

He turns to face a massive oak tree, one that stands tall and proud in the middle of the clearing. Without a moment's hesitation, he steps forward, his hands wrapping around the trunk. He pulls, and the earth groans as the tree's roots snap like thick ropes. The sound of cracking wood fills the air as Ryker lifts the entire tree from the ground, holding it above his head like it's weightless.

My breath catches in my throat.

"Your turn," Ryker says to Eira, tossing the tree aside like it's a twig.

Eira looks stunned but takes a deep breath. She steps toward another tree, smaller than the one Ryker uprooted, but still imposing. She places her hands on the trunk and focuses, her brow furrowed in concentration.

At first, nothing happens, but then I see the roots start to give way, dirt loosening as Eira pulls with all her might. The tree creaks and groans before finally snapping free. Eira stumbles back as the massive trunk crashes to the ground.

"I did it," she says, her voice shaking with excitement.

Ryker smiles at her, his pride evident. "Good. But remember, with power like this, comes responsibility. You have to control it."

I watch Eira, her triumph glowing on her face, and I can't help but feel a wave of awe—mixed with something else. Something deeper, darker. The raw power on display is staggering, and I find myself wondering just how much I'm missing. The power to do this—to control it, to bend the world to your will—*what would that feel like?*

But more than that, I think of the moment when I siphoned power from Ryker. At the time, I didn't understand it, didn't even know it was possible. But now, watching him, feeling the weight of his abilities, it all clicks into place.

He's not human. Not entirely. And I am connected to that power. How much of me is me anymore?

The training session comes to an end, the night air growing colder as we prepare to leave the clearing. Eira looks exhausted but exhilarated, her confidence soaring after the session.

"Ryker," I say quietly, taking a step toward him. He turns to face me, his eyes dark but softening at the sound of my voice.

"I just... I wanted to thank you," I say, my words catching in my throat. "For helping Eira. And I'm sorry for how I acted before. I didn't understand."

He looks at me for a long moment, his expression unreadable. Then, to my surprise, he steps forward and pulls me into an embrace.

I freeze, the shock of his sudden closeness making my breath catch in my chest. But then something inside me breaks. The weight of everything—the fear, the anger, the confusion— dissipates, and I let myself lean into him.

"It's okay," he murmurs. "I deserved that. And I'm sorry, too. For not telling you the truth sooner."

I don't know how long we stand there, but for the first time in days, I feel like I'm not alone in this. I feel like, maybe, I don't have to carry this burden on my own anymore.

As we make our way back to the Academy, the night no longer feels so heavy. Eira's voice is light with excitement as she recounts everything she's learned. Ryker walks ahead of us, his figure a silhouette in the moonlight. I follow behind, my mind racing with all the new things I've learned tonight, but a small, fragile sense of peace settles in my chest.

I don't have all the answers yet. But for the first time in a long while, I feel like I'm heading in the right direction.

And maybe, for now, that's enough.

# 23

# Vervainy magic

I don't know how to explain it. Watching Eira adapt to her new reality has been both inspiring and infuriating. She's getting stronger every day, learning to control the hunger, the instincts that come with being a vampire. And while I'm proud of her, I can't ignore the way it gnaws at me.

I have powers too—abilities that are growing every day, threatening to consume me. And what am I doing about it? Nothing. Watching from the sidelines while everyone else figures out their own strengths. It's unbearable.

"Neville, I need to talk to you." My voice comes out sharper than I mean it to as I find him in the common room. He's reading—of course he is. He barely even looks up as I approach.

"About what?" he asks, flipping a page lazily.

"Neville, I need you to teach me." The words tumble out of my mouth faster than I intended, but I can't take them back now. They hang in the air between us, weighty and unrelenting.

Neville looks up from his book, eyebrows raised in that

maddeningly calm way of his, like he already knows what I'm about to say. But he doesn't know. Not really. He has no idea how desperately I need this.

"Teach you what?" His voice is measured, but there's a thread of hesitation, like he already wants to refuse.

I cross my arms and take a step closer. "How to control my powers. How to use them." My voice is firmer than I expected, but that's good. I need him to see how serious I am.

Neville sighs, closing his book and setting it aside. Of course, he doesn't take me seriously right away. "Asterine, you don't know what you're asking for. Your powers aren't like the others'. They're dangerous. If you lose control—"

"Then what?" I cut him off, the frustration bubbling to the surface. "What's the worst that can happen? I hurt someone? I ruin everything? Neville, I'm already losing control, and I'm barely even using my powers. At least if you teach me, I'll have a chance to manage it. To stop being afraid."

He leans back in his chair, rubbing his temples. "Asterine, you're not ready for this."

"I'm never going to be ready if I don't start." My voice wavers, and I take a deep breath, trying to steady it. "This is who I am, Neville. I can feel it growing inside me. Every day, it gets stronger, and I can't ignore it anymore. You have to help me."

There's a long pause, and for a moment, I think he's going to say no. But then he sighs, standing up and facing me.

"Also you owe me, for lying to my face and for everything else" I mutter at him. As much as I want to hate him, he's my twin and he's given me enough reasons behind his actions. I don't justify them, any of them but right now there is nothing much in my hands when I really need his help.

"Alright, fine." His tone is reluctant, but I can see the flicker of determination in his eyes. "But we're doing this my way. No shortcuts. No taking risks you're not ready for. You'll listen to everything I say."

Relief washes over me, and I nod quickly. "Thank you."

He looks at me for a moment longer, his expression softening slightly. "Meet me in the clearing today evening. I'll bring the others. They should see this too."

"The others? Why?" My stomach twists at the thought of having an audience.

"Because you're part of this group, Asterine, whether you like it or not. They need to know what you're capable of. And maybe you need to know it too."

The clearing feels impossibly vast when I step into it this evening. The trees rise high around us, their branches forming a canopy that filters the dusk into orangey patterns on the ground. The air is cool, carrying the faint scent of damp earth and leaves. I tug my jacket tighter around me, my nerves coiling tighter with every step.

To my horror, the entire group is already here. Eira, Ryker, Maeve, Fabian, and Jocosa stand in a loose circle, their faces lit by the pale rays of the sunset. Why did Neville have to bring all of them? The weight of their gazes makes my skin prickle.

I mutter under my breath as I step into the clearing. "It's not a big deal. Why do they all have to watch?"

Neville smirks, clearly overhearing me. "You'll be fine. Just focus on what you're here to do."

That's easier said than done. I can feel every pair of eyes on me, scrutinizing, judging. Even Ryker, leaning casually against a tree, manages to make me feel like I'm under a microscope. His midnight-black eyes catch the sunrays, glinting like polished obsidian, and for a brief moment, I wonder what he's thinking. Probably that I'm about to embarrass myself.

"Alright, Asterine, let's start with the basics." Neville's voice pulls me back to the moment. He gestures to a small plant growing near the edge of the clearing, its dark green leaves shimmering faintly in the light. "This is vervain."

The name sends a ripple of tension through the group. I glance at Eira, whose expression has tightened, her jaw set. Ryker straightens slightly, his casual demeanor replaced by something sharper, more alert.

"Vervain is a mystical plant," Neville explains, his tone calm but firm. "It's used by witches for protection, but it's also deadly to vampires."

At that, Ryker's expression darkens. "You brought vervain here? Seriously?"

Neville nods, unfazed. "It's the perfect way to teach Asterine. She needs to understand the kind of power she's dealing with." What does he mean? Deadly to vampires? I have been just revealed a few weeks ago of mystical creatures and now plants? the literal nature too? Wow.

"Ryker, please come here" Nev voices.

"I'm not touching that thing," Ryker mutters, crossing his arms like a scared baby. He looks so cute when he's doing this, I almost smile. *Focus Asterine.*

Neville steps closer, holding out the plant. "I'm not asking you to hold it. Just help me demonstrate." My twin brother is literally asking a vampire to hold vervain. Only Neville could be as persuasive as he is. I don't dare to speak in between them to express my concerns for Ryker and get stuck is crossfire, especially since Nev told me we were doing things his way.

Ryker glares at him, his jaw tightening. For a moment, I

think he's going to refuse outright, but then he sighs, stepping forward reluctantly. "Fine. But if this goes wrong, I'm blaming you."

Neville smirks, holding the vervain carefully. He brushes the leaves against Ryker's arm, and the reaction is immediate. Ryker flinches, his teeth clenching as his skin begins to redden and blister. I watch, horrified, as the vervain burns him, the damage spreading like wildfire.

But then when Neville retreats the vervain off his arm, just as quickly, the burns vanish. Ryker's skin starts to heal in seconds, the blisters retreating until there's no trace of them left. The sight is both fascinating and unsettling. From what I have knows in the past few days I know vampires are fast healers but this fast? Damn.

"That's the power of vervain," Neville says, turning to me. "Now it's your turn. Touch the plant and see if you can sense the magic within it. Siphoning isn't just about taking power—it's about recognizing it first."

I hesitate, staring at the plant in Neville's hand. It looks so small, so harmless, but I know better now. I take a deep breath, stepping forward and reaching out. My fingers brush against the leaves, and I feel it instantly—a faint hum, like an electric current running through my veins.

I close my eyes, focusing on the sensation. The magic in the plant is alive, thrumming with energy. Slowly, I reach for it, trying to pull it toward me. It resists at first, but then it begins to flow, the power slipping into me like a warm stream. The more I pull, the stronger the sensation becomes, until finally, the hum fades, leaving the plant empty in my hand.

When I open my eyes, Neville is watching me closely, a flicker of pride in his gaze. "Good. Now let's test it." Ryker flinches at that statement and I almost feel sorry for him. Poor guy must be so scared of that little plant. I don't know the idea of Ryker being afraid of a small plant kind of seems to funny to me but it's not when you know what Ryker is and what vervain does exactly to him.

He takes the now-drained vervain and brushes it against Ryker's arm again. This time, nothing happens. Ryker looks down at his un-burnt skin, his expression one of surprise—and something else I can't quite name.

"It doesn't hurt," he mutters, his voice low.

The others exchange glances, their shock palpable. I can feel the weight of their stares, but this time, it doesn't bother me. I did that.

"Now, let's see if you can use the power you've siphoned," Neville says, placing a bundle of dry leaves on the ground. "Try to light these."

He doesn't tell me what to do and how to do it but as from what I know back my dorm room when I messed up with Eira's bed the night Neville was back and how I undid what I did was just like thinking about it and then it happening. So, I try to test the same theory here.

I nod, my confidence growing. I close my eyes again, reaching for the energy inside me. It feels warm and alive, like a fire waiting to be unleashed. I focus on the leaves, imagining the power flowing from me into them. At first, nothing happens. My face falls because I surely felt something going and just as I start to question myself, slowly, a spark flickers to life, and within seconds, the leaves are burning brightly. It's all about having patience which for me seems really and utterly arduous.

The clearing falls silent, everyone watching the flames with wide eyes. I step back, my chest heaving, the thrill of what I've just done coursing through me.

"Well done, Asterine," Neville says, his voice filled with pride. I already feel better to be able to do something with myself other than overthink and sulk. It honestly feels like when you workout and don't feel lethargic anymore rather feel more pumped. I know and acknowledge it's just the start but it is something instead of nothing. My mood is better after ages.

Later, as the others start to leave, I find myself walking toward Ryker, who's standing at the edge of the clearing. He looks at me, his expression unreadable, but there's something softer in his gaze. I have missed looking at his face the time when I was ignoring him. Seems like it wasn't a good idea now but I am stubborn even when it's my loss.

"I'm sorry for earlier," I say, my voice quiet. "For burning you."

He smirks, his copper hair catching the now pale moonlight. "Don't worry about it. I've had worse. But I have to admit, you're pretty impressive."

His words make my heart skip a beat, and for a moment, I forget how to breathe. "You're not so bad yourself," I manage to say, though my voice is barely above a whisper.

The tension between us feels different now, charged with something I can't quite name. But before I can overthink it, he gives me a small, almost playful smile and walks away, leaving me standing there, feeling both lighter and more confused than ever.

# 24

# Shifts in the Air

I watch Ryker disappear into the trees, his copper hair catching the moonlight one last time before he vanishes from sight. My heart is still pounding, my cheeks warm with a blush that refuses to fade. What just happened?

I touch my arm absentmindedly, the ghost of where his hand brushed mine still lingering. "You're pretty impressive," he'd said. The words replay in my mind, and I feel a small, giddy smile tugging at my lips before I can stop it. What is happening to me?

I've never felt like this before. Lighter, almost… giddy? It's ridiculous, really. But at the same time, I can't help but hold on to that moment. It felt… nice. Too nice. Stop it, Asterine. You've got enough to deal with. I shake my head, trying to clear the thoughts, but they linger like a stubborn echo.

"Asterine, you coming?" Neville's voice snaps me out of my daze, and I turn to see him and the others waiting for me at the edge of the clearing. His expression is curious but guarded, like he knows something's shifted but isn't ready to ask about it yet.

"Yeah, right behind you," I call out, jogging to catch up with them. Eira falls into step beside Neville, and I can't help but notice how easily they talk now, their laughter low and easy as they exchange some inside joke I'm not privy to. A strange pang settles in my chest, but I push it aside.

"You okay?" Eira asks, glancing at me with those sharp, clear eyes of hers. She looks so much better now—more at ease, more herself. It's like she's found her footing, even in the chaos of her new reality.

"Better than okay," I admit, unable to keep the small smile off my face. "I think tonight went well."

"It did," she agrees, a knowing smile playing on her lips. "You were great out there, Asterine. Even Ryker thought so."

My blush deepens, and I look away quickly. "He didn't say that."

"Sure, he didn't," she teases, her tone light. "But it's written all over your face."

I don't respond, my cheeks burning too hot to risk saying anything that might give me away. Instead, I quicken my pace, leaving them behind as I walk back toward the dorms.

The next few days pass in a blur of classes, training, and a newfound sense of confidence that surprises even me. For the first time since coming to Harlow Academy, I feel like I'm finding my place. I'm doing better in school—actually keeping up with my assignments and even answering questions in class. Who knew all it took was a little bit of magical training to turn my life around?

But it's not just the academic progress that has me feeling bubbly. It's the way everything seems to be falling into place. My powers are becoming easier to control with Neville's guidance, and our training sessions have become a routine

I actually look forward to.

Of course, Eira is always there, sitting cross-legged on the grass with her sharp vampire senses picking up every detail of our sessions. At first, I thought she was just there out of curiosity, but it's become clear that she's there for Neville as much as she is for me.

The way they interact now—it's hard not to notice. The way her laugh softens around him, the way his usually stoic demeanor breaks into a grin when she teases him—it's enough to make anyone suspicious. And honestly? I think it's sweet.

"Eira, do you ever get bored watching us?" I ask during one of our sessions, half-joking as I try to siphon energy from the earth. Nature also has energy which I recently found out due to Neville.

She shrugs, her lips quirking into a smirk. "Not really. It's fun watching you struggle."

"Gee, thanks," I mutter, rolling my eyes.

Neville chuckles, shaking his head. "She's just here to make sure I don't go easy on you."

"Oh, is that what this is?" I shoot back, trying to hide my grin.

But when I glance at Eira again, her attention isn't on me anymore. She's watching Neville, her expression softening in a way that makes my chest ache—not with jealousy, but with a strange sense of relief. She's found someone she trusts, someone who grounds her in a way I never could. And maybe that's okay.

One afternoon, I find myself alone in the library, flipping through books on magical theory. My progress in controlling my powers has been steady, but there's still so much I don't understand about what I can do. Why didn't my parents ever tell me about this? About what I am?

The thought gnaws at me, but I try to focus on the task at hand. I'm just starting to make sense of a particularly dense passage when a voice cuts through my concentration.

"Doing some light reading?"

I glance up to see Ryker leaning casually against the bookshelf, his midnight-black eyes glinting with amusement. My heart does that annoying little flutter again, and I force myself to look away quickly.

"Just trying to figure out what I'm doing," I say, keeping my tone as neutral as possible. "Not all of us are born knowing how to handle our powers."

"Fair enough," he says, pushing off the shelf and coming to sit across from me. "You're doing better than I expected, though. Neville's a good teacher."

"He is," I agree, surprised by the warmth in his voice. "But I still have a long way to go."

Ryker shrugs, his smirk softening into something almost... genuine. "You'll get there. You're tougher than you look."

I don't know what to say to that, so I just nod, trying to ignore the way my cheeks are heating up again. What is it about him that gets under my skin so easily?

That evening, during another training session, Neville has me working on controlling the energy I siphon. The power hums under my skin, alive and restless, but I'm getting better at directing it.

"Good, Asterine," Neville says, his voice encouraging. "Now focus. Channel it into the spell."

I close my eyes, focusing on the small flame in front of me. Slowly, I feed it the energy, watching as it grows brighter and steadier. It's exhilarating, but also a little terrifying. Is this what power feels like?

When I open my eyes, Eira is grinning at me from her spot on the grass. "Told you you'd get the hang of it."

"Don't jinx it," I warn, but I can't help but smile back.

As we wrap up the session, Neville walks Eira back toward the dorms, their voices fading into the night. I watch them go, a strange mix of emotions swirling in my chest. But then I feel someone step up beside me, and I don't even have to look to know who it is.

"You've come a long way," Ryker says, his voice low and steady.

"Thanks," I say softly, glancing up at him. His copper hair glints in the moonlight, and his midnight-black eyes are unreadable, but there's something in his expression that makes my heart skip.

For a moment, we just stand there, the silence stretching between us. And then, out of nowhere, he says, "You know, you're kind of amazing when you're not overthinking everything."

The words catch me off guard, and I feel my cheeks heat up again. "I don't—what does that even mean?"

He chuckles, stepping back. "You'll figure it out." And just like that, he's gone, leaving me standing there with a heart that's suddenly racing and a blush I can't shake.

<h1 style="text-align:center">25</h1>

# The old Basement Library

I lie awake in bed, staring at the ceiling. Eira's soft breathing fills the room, a steady rhythm that should be soothing, but tonight it's anything but. My thoughts are restless, swirling with the remnants of the power still buzzing under my skin. Neville doesn't know I held on to some of it. No one does.

I can feel it—alive, thrumming just beneath the surface, begging to be used. I know I should let it go, let it dissipate like Neville taught me. But something about it feels… right. Like it belongs to me.

I glance over at Eira, sound asleep, then slip out of bed as quietly as I can. My feet barely make a sound as I tiptoe to the door, the cool wood pressing against my palms as I open it. The hallway is silent, the dim light from the moon filtering through the tall Gothic windows casting long, eerie shadows on the stone walls.

I don't know what compels me to go to the basement library. Maybe it's the lingering energy in my veins, or maybe it's the memory of being down there before, during the chaos with

Evander. Something about that place has always felt… alive. Like it's waiting for something—or someone.

My heart pounds as I make my way through the dark corridors, the air growing cooler with each step. The castle-like structure of Harlow Academy creaks around me, the sound of my own breathing amplified in the silence. Every creak of the wooden floorboards makes me glance over my shoulder, but the hallways remain empty. Why does this feel like a bad idea?

I finally reach the heavy door that leads to the basement library. The air here is thicker, colder, carrying with it the faint scent of old parchment and dust. I push the door open, the groan of the hinges echoing in the stillness. The stairs leading down are steep and narrow, but I take them two at a time, my pulse quickening with anticipation.

The basement library is just as I remember it: ancient, crumbling, and coated in layers of dust. Shelves stand tall but warped, their edges sagging under the weight of centuries-old books. Spiderwebs stretch like fragile threads across the room, glinting faintly in the flickering light of a few candles I light as I step further inside. Shadows dance across the stone walls, giving the place an almost otherworldly feel.

I take a deep breath, letting the charged air fill my lungs. It feels different down here, like the magic in the library is alive, humming faintly in the background. This is the perfect place to try what I've been wanting to do since I read about it.

I pull a chair into the center of the room, clearing a small space for myself. My eyes fall on the scattered books and crumbling papers littering the floor. So much chaos, so much potential. I close my eyes and focus, reaching for the power still thrumming inside me. It feels warm, almost electric, a steady pulse that's both comforting and exhilarating.

In one of the books I'd read about siphoners, there was a passage about manipulating objects with magic—about channeling energy outward, using it to move and control things without ever touching them. It seemed impossible then. But now? Now, I know it's not.

I stretch out my hands, palms up, and focus on the scattered books around me. I picture them rising, their weight lifting from the floor, and push the magic outward, willing it to obey. At first, nothing happens. The air remains still, the books lying motionless like stubborn children refusing to cooperate.

But then, something shifts. I feel the power surge through me, filling the room like a sudden gust of wind. The books tremble, their covers shaking as if responding to my call. My breath catches in my throat as, one by one, they rise into the air, hovering several feet above the ground.

A grin spreads across my face, pride swelling in my chest. I did it. I actually did it.

The books begin to spin slowly, forming a gentle circle above me. I let out a breath I didn't realize I was holding, the power in my veins flowing freely now, more natural than it's ever felt before. The candles flicker wildly, their flames dancing in time with the movement of the books.

I watch in awe as the books continue to spin, faster and faster, their edges blurring into a whirlwind of paper and magic. The air grows heavier, charged with energy, and I can feel the room itself responding to the power I've unleashed. The shelves groan, the stone walls trembling faintly, as if the entire library is alive and listening.

Carefully, I guide the books back to their shelves, watching as they settle into place with a satisfying thud. The room stills, the energy receding like a tide, leaving behind an eerie silence. I lower my hands, my chest heaving with exertion but my heart bursting with pride. I've never felt so powerful.

I glance around the room, taking in the neatly arranged shelves and the faint glow of the candles. The library looks different now—less chaotic, more orderly. More alive.

As I turn to blow out the candles and leave, a sudden force slams into me, sending me sprawling across the floor. Pain shoots through my side as I collide with the hard stone, the air knocked from my lungs. For a moment, I'm too stunned to move, my mind racing to process what just happened.

I sit up slowly, my heart hammering against my ribs. The candles flicker wildly, their flames casting frantic shadows across the walls. I strain to listen, but the library is silent, save for the sound of my own ragged breathing. *What the hell was that?*

"Hello?" My voice comes out shakier than I intended, echoing in the empty space. No response.

I push myself to my feet, wincing at the dull ache in my ribs. My eyes scan the room, searching for any sign of what— or who—hit me. But the library is empty, the shadows still dancing like they're mocking me.

I take a cautious step forward, every instinct screaming at me to run. But something keeps me rooted in place, my curiosity warring with my fear. I reach out with my magic, searching for any trace of energy, but the power I felt moments ago is gone, leaving behind an unsettling emptiness.

And then, I hear it—a faint whisper, so soft I almost think I imagined it. It's coming from deeper in the library, from the darkened corner where the shelves seem to lean in on themselves. The sound sends a shiver down my spine, my pulse quickening as I take a hesitant step toward it.

"Who's there?" My voice echoes again, and this time, the whisper stops. The silence that follows is deafening, pressing down on me like a physical weight.

Before I can take another step, something moves—a blur of shadow darting across the edge of my vision. I whip around, my magic flaring instinctively, but there's nothing there. Just the flickering candles and the steady creak of the old wooden shelves.

My breath comes faster now, my chest tight with panic. Whatever's here, it's not friendly. I can feel it—a cold, malevolent presence that seems to linger just out of sight, watching, waiting.

I take a step back, then another, my hands trembling as I reach for the nearest candle. The flame flickers as I blow it out, plunging that corner of the room into darkness. The shadows seem to shift again, closer this time, and I turn to run.

But before I can make it to the stairs, something slams into me again, harder this time. I hit the ground with a cry, my vision swimming as pain radiates through my body. My magic flares wildly, uncontrolled, but it does nothing to stop whatever's coming.

# 26

# Vancy Fancy

The pain in my ribs throbs as I press my hands against the cold stone floor, trying to push myself upright. My arms tremble, refusing to cooperate. I can barely move, let alone stand, and the room around me tilts as my vision wavers. I squeeze my eyes shut, forcing myself to take shallow breaths, but my chest feels like it's caving in.

When I finally manage to lift my head, I see him. A figure standing a few feet away, his silhouette sharp against the flickering candlelight. He takes a step closer, and as the light touches his face, I feel my stomach drop.

He's pale, almost unnaturally so, his skin like porcelain stretched too thin. His bright, predatory eyes gleam with an unnatural light, and his mouth curls into a smirk that makes my skin crawl. His sharp features are shadowed, his messy hair framing a face that's both unnervingly beautiful and utterly terrifying.

"Well, well," he says, his voice low and smooth, with a thick British accent that sends a shiver down my spine. "What a sorry state you're in, love."

My breath catches, and I press myself back against the nearest shelf, trying to put as much distance as I can between us. "Who—who are you?" My voice comes out weak, barely audible, but it's the only sound I can manage.

He tilts his head, the smirk never leaving his face. "Vance," he says simply, as if the name alone should answer all my questions. His accent lingers on the word, sharp and deliberate, like he's savoring it. "You might say I've been keeping an eye on you."

I force myself to sit up, my arms still trembling. "What do you want?"

"Straight to the point. I like that." He takes another step closer, his movements smooth and deliberate, like a predator stalking its prey. "It's not about what I want, darling. It's about what my queen wants."

"Your... queen?" My voice falters, and I swallow hard, trying to keep the rising panic at bay.

"Oh yes," he says, his smirk widening. "She's quite keen on meeting you. You're something of a... curiosity."

I shake my head, my heart pounding so hard it feels like it's going to burst. "I'm not going anywhere with you."

His laugh is soft but chilling, echoing in the stillness of the library. "Oh, I think you are. You see, I don't leave empty-handed. And as for your little friend—Eira, was it?—you can thank me for her transformation."

The mention of Eira sends a jolt of anger through me, momentarily overriding my fear. "You bit her. You turned her into—"

"A masterpiece," Vance interrupts, his smirk sharpening. "She's exquisite, isn't she? A perfect fledgling, though I suppose she's struggling a bit. Such a pity I couldn't stay to help her through it."

My hands clench into fists, my magic sparking faintly beneath my skin. "You're a monster."

"Careful, little siphoner," he says, his voice dropping to a warning growl. "You're not in any position to make accusations."

The word siphoner sends another jolt through me, this time of cold dread. He knows what I am. How does he know? My mind races, searching for an escape, but before I can think of anything, he moves.

In an instant, he's in front of me, his hand closing around my arm with a grip like iron. I gasp, struggling against him, but he doesn't even flinch. "I'd rather not make a mess of this," he says, his voice calm but laced with menace. "But I will if I have to."

"No!" I scream, kicking and clawing at him, but it's like fighting against a steel wall. He hauls me to my feet effortlessly, his smirk never wavering.

"Shh, love," he murmurs, his British accent making the words sound almost mocking. "No need to make a fuss. You'll thank me later."

He drags me across the library, my feet barely touching the ground as I struggle against him. My chest heaves, my breath coming in short, panicked gasps. I catch a flicker of movement ahead and feel my stomach twist.

At the far end of the library, something shimmers—a glowing circle, its edges crackling with energy. It pulses faintly, a swirling mass of deep purples and blacks that shift and churn like storm clouds caught in an endless spiral. The air around it is heavy, vibrating with power, and I feel a sickening pull toward it, like it's alive and hungry.

"What is that?" I whisper, my voice trembling.

"That, my dear," Vance says, his tone almost cheerful, "is our ticket out of here."

"No," I breathe, shaking my head. "No, I'm not going in there."

He chuckles, the sound low and sinister. "You don't have much of a choice."

I dig my heels into the ground, my magic sparking again as I try to pull away, but his grip tightens painfully. The closer we get to the portal, the stronger the pull becomes, like it's trying to swallow me whole. My heart races, my mind screaming at me to fight, to do something, but my body feels weak, uncooperative.

"Let her go."

The voice is sharp, commanding, and instantly recognizable. My head snaps toward the sound, and relief floods through me like a tidal wave.

"Ryker," I whisper, my voice barely audible.

He stands at the entrance to the library, his stance rigid, his midnight-black eyes locked on Vance. His copper hair glints faintly in the dim light, and there's a fire in his gaze I've never seen before—pure, unrelenting fury.

"Well, if it isn't the hero," Vance says, turning slightly to face him. "You're just in time to say goodbye."

"Let her go," Ryker repeats, his voice low and dangerous.

Vance smirks, his grip on my arm unrelenting. "And what exactly are you going to do about it?"

"I'll rip you apart if you don't," Ryker growls, taking a step closer. His movements are controlled, deliberate, but I can see the tension in his body, the way his fists clench at his sides.

"Brave words," Vance says, his tone mocking. "But I'm afraid you're a bit late to the party."

Before Ryker can react, Vance moves. He steps into the portal, dragging me with him, and the world around us dissolves into chaos.

The swirling energy pulls at me, cold and suffocating, as we're yanked through the vortex. The air feels like it's being torn from my lungs, the colors and shapes around me blurring into a nauseating whirl. My chest burns, my heart pounding erratically as the portal's pull grows stronger, dragging us deeper into its endless void.

When we land, it's with a jarring thud that sends pain shooting through my body. The ground beneath me is cold and unyielding, the air damp and heavy with the metallic tang of blood. My head spins as I try to sit up, my limbs trembling from the effort.

Vance releases me, stepping back with an infuriatingly smug grin. "Welcome to your new home, love."

I look around, my heart sinking as I take in my surroundings. The darkness here is suffocating, pressing in on all sides, broken only by faint, flickering lights that cast eerie shadows on the stone walls. The air is thick, stifling, and every instinct screams at me to run.

But there's nowhere to go.

## 27

# Caged

The world around me is a haze of shadows and cold. My body aches, my ribs screaming with every shallow breath as I'm dragged through the suffocating darkness. Vance's grip on my arm is unrelenting, his pace brisk and unforgiving. The air here is heavy, damp, and filled with the metallic tang of something unidentifiable. My feet scrape against the stone floor, every step feeling heavier than the last.

"Welcome to the queen's domain," Vance says, his thick British accent laced with mockery. He doesn't even look at me as he speaks, his tone casual, almost conversational. "You'll find it… unforgettable."

I can barely focus on his words, the pain in my chest and the swirling nausea from the portal still gripping me tightly. My head pounds, my thoughts fractured and chaotic. What have I gotten myself into? How am I going to get out of this?

The corridor we're in seems to stretch forever, its walls jagged and uneven, like the earth itself has been carved out and forced to serve as a prison. The faint glow of torches lines the walls, their flickering light casting long, shifting shadows that make everything feel alive. The cold seeps into my skin, biting and unrelenting.

As we turn a corner, two figures emerge from the shadows ahead. They're tall and imposing, their faces hidden by dark hoods. The air around them feels wrong, charged with an energy that makes my skin crawl. My pulse quickens as they approach, their presence suffocating.

"This is her?" one of them asks, his voice low and gravelly.

Vance nods, his smirk widening. "The siphoner herself. Isn't she lovely?"

I try to pull away, but Vance's grip tightens, and I gasp as pain shoots through my arm. "Let me go," I manage to choke out, my voice trembling.

"Feisty," the other figure says, his tone laced with amusement. "That won't last long."

Before I can respond, one of them steps forward, holding something in his hands. The faint light catches on it, and my breath hitches. It's a chain, but not just any chain—its surface glints unnaturally, shifting with a faint, iridescent sheen that makes my stomach churn.

"What is that?" I whisper, my voice barely audible.

"You'll find out soon enough," Vance says, his tone almost cheerful.

The chain is cold as ice when it touches my skin, and the effect is immediate. A wave of nausea crashes over me, and I stumble, my legs buckling beneath me. The buzzing warmth of my magic, always present like a second heartbeat, vanishes in an instant. I gasp, clutching at my chest as the emptiness consumes me.

"What... what did you do?" I whisper, my voice trembling.

Vance crouches in front of me, his bright eyes glinting with satisfaction. "Mystic metal," he says, his tone dripping with smugness. "Drains every ounce of magic from you. Keeps you nice and harmless."

I try to push him away, but my strength is gone. My arms feel like lead, my entire body weighed down by the oppressive cold of the chains. I can barely lift my head as the figures pull me to my feet, their grip rough and unyielding.

"Move," one of them orders, shoving me forward.

I stumble, the chains rattling around me as I'm forced to walk. Every step feels heavier than the last, the weight of the chains dragging me down. My head spins, my thoughts a chaotic mess. How did I let this happen? How could I be so careless?

The corridor opens up into a massive chamber, its walls lined with cells. The air is thick with despair, the distant sound of chains clinking and muffled cries echoing through the space. Torches flicker weakly, casting long shadows that stretch across the uneven floor. The smell of damp stone and decay fills my nose, and I have to fight the urge to retch.

"This will do," one of the figures says, gesturing to an empty cell at the far end of the chamber.

They shove me forward, and I stumble again, falling to my knees as they unlock the heavy iron door. My palms scrape against the rough stone floor, and I bite back a cry of pain. My magic, my strength—everything feels so far away, like a part of me has been ripped out and left behind.

"Inside," one of them barks, grabbing me by the arm and hauling me to my feet.

I don't resist this time. What's the point? I'm too weak, too drained to fight back. They push me into the cell, the door slamming shut behind me with a deafening clang. The sound reverberates through the chamber, echoing in my ears like a death knell.

"Rest up," Vance says, his smirk audible even from behind the bars. "The queen will see you soon."

I glare at him, anger and fear swirling in my chest, but I don't say anything. What can I say? He's already won. He turns and walks away, his laugh fading into the distance as the figures follow him, leaving me alone in the suffocating silence.

I slump against the cold stone wall, the chains still heavy around my wrists. The emptiness inside me is unbearable, a hollow ache where my magic used to be. Is this what it feels like to be powerless? To have everything you are stripped away?

Tears prick at the corners of my eyes, but I blink them away, refusing to let them fall. Crying won't help. Nothing will. I wrap my arms around my knees, pulling them close to my chest as I try to steady my breathing. The walls of the cell seem to close in around me, the darkness pressing down like a weight I can't escape.

My mind races, jumping from one thought to the next. What does the queen want with me? What's her plan? Is there any way out of this?

I think of Eira, of Neville, of Ryker. Do they even know I'm gone? Will they come looking for me? A bitter laugh escapes my lips at the thought. Of course they will. But will they find me in time?

The chains around my wrists dig into my skin, their cold bite a constant reminder of my helplessness. I close my eyes, trying to focus, to reach for even the faintest spark of my magic, but there's nothing. Just emptiness.

I take a shaky breath, the air catching in my throat. I can't give up. Not like this.

But as the minutes stretch into hours, the silence pressing down like a physical weight, the flicker of hope in my chest begins to fade.

# 28

# Reunion

The chains bite into my wrists as I'm hauled through the dark corridors, the echo of my footsteps drowned by the heavy boots of the guards flanking me. My heart pounds against my ribs, a relentless rhythm of fear and anger. Every step feels heavier than the last, the weight of the mystic metal sapping what little strength I have left.

When the double doors ahead creak open, I catch my first glimpse of the court. My breath catches in my throat. The room is massive, its vaulted ceiling stretching so high it seems to disappear into darkness. Columns carved with intricate, otherworldly patterns line the space, their surfaces glowing faintly with an eerie light. The air is thick, humming with an oppressive energy that makes my skin crawl.

At the far end of the room, a throne sits atop a raised dais. It's unlike anything I've ever seen—carved from a dark, glossy stone that seems to drink in the light around it, its surface etched with glowing runes. The very sight of it makes my stomach churn.

I'm shoved forward, my knees buckling as I'm forced into

the center of the room. The guards release me, stepping back but staying close enough to block any attempt at escape. I struggle to stand, my legs trembling beneath me, but before I can find my balance, my eyes land on the figures standing at the edges of the court.

My breath hitches. "No…"

Ryker. Eira. Neville. They're all here.

Eira's pale face is twisted in fear and anger, her hands clenching at her sides as though she's fighting the urge to lunge at the guards. Neville stands beside her, his jaw tight, his eyes scanning the room like he's searching for a way out. And Ryker—his midnight-black eyes are locked on me, his expression unreadable, but the tension in his body is palpable.

"What are you doing here?" My voice cracks, barely audible over the hum of the room.

"We came to save you," Neville says, his tone laced with frustration. "Clearly, it didn't go as planned."

My chest tightens, a mix of relief and dread flooding through me. They came for me. But now they're here, trapped like I am, and the guilt crashes over me like a wave. This is my fault. I should never have left the dorm, never gone to the library, never—

A sudden hush falls over the room, and my thoughts scatter like leaves in the wind. The air grows heavier, colder, as if the very space is holding its breath. And then, she enters.

The Queen.

She moves with an unnatural grace, her figure draped in dark, flowing robes that shimmer faintly as she walks. Her face is striking, impossibly beautiful and yet sharp enough to cut. Her eyes, a piercing shade of violet, sweep over the room, their intensity sending a shiver down my spine. Her presence is suffocating, commanding, as though the very world bends to her will.

But it's not her appearance that makes the blood drain from my face. It's the way Ryker stiffens, his breath catching audibly as she approaches.

"Mother..." he breathes, his voice barely above a whisper.

I blink, my mind reeling. Mother? The Queen is Ryker's mother?

The revelation slams into me like a physical blow, my thoughts spinning out of control. Ryker, who's always been so guarded about his past, so reluctant to share anything about his family—this is what he's been hiding? His mother is the Queen of whatever hellish realm we've been dragged into?

She stops before us, her violet eyes locking onto Ryker with a cold intensity that makes my blood run cold. "Ryker," she says, her voice smooth and commanding. "How... predictable."

"Let them go," Ryker says, his voice steadier now, though his fists clench at his sides. "This has nothing to do with them."

"Oh, but it has everything to do with them," she replies, a faint smirk playing on her lips. "And with you."

Before anyone can respond, another figure steps forward from the shadows behind her. My heart skips a beat as recognition slams into me.

Evander.

He looks just as he did the last time I saw him—tall, imposing, his sharp features marred only by the cruel smirk that twists his lips. His sea-green eyes, once so captivating, now gleam with a malice that sends a chill down my spine. The siren from the first book. The man who almost destroyed us all.

"Miss me?" he drawls, his voice smooth and mocking.

My legs threaten to give out beneath me, but I force myself

to stand tall, even as my body trembles. "You…" The word escapes my lips in a breathless whisper, a mix of anger and fear.

"Surprised to see me?" he asks, his smirk widening. "I'll admit, I wasn't sure you'd survive our last encounter. But you've proven to be… resilient."

"Evander…" Ryker's voice is low, dangerous, and I can see the way his entire body tenses, like he's ready to attack at any moment. "What are you doing here?"

Evander tilts his head, his smirk never faltering. "Isn't it obvious? I'm home."

My mind races, struggling to make sense of what's happening. Evander is here. Ryker's mother is the Queen. And we're all trapped in her court, powerless and surrounded by enemies. How did it come to this? How are we supposed to get out of this?

"Enough," the Queen says, her voice cutting through the tension like a knife. She turns her gaze to me, and I feel the weight of her scrutiny, like she's peeling back every layer of my being and exposing my very soul. "So, you're the siphoner everyone's been whispering about."

I want to speak, to deny it, to demand answers, but the words stick in my throat. Her presence is overwhelming, suffocating, and I can barely breathe under the weight of her gaze.

"She's nothing special," Evander says, his tone dismissive. "Just a girl with a bit of borrowed power."

The Queen's lips curl into a faint smile. "We'll see."

Her words send a chill down my spine, and I struggle to hold back the fear threatening to consume me. This is it. This is how it ends.

But as the silence stretches on, a flicker of defiance sparks in my chest. I may be powerless now, but I won't let them see me break. Not yet. Not ever.

## 29

# Family and Betrayal

The air in the Queen's court feels heavier, more oppressive, as if the very room is feeding off the tension swirling between all of us. My body aches from the weight of the mystic chains, but the sight of Evander and the Queen standing side by side has rooted me to the spot. It's too much, too surreal, like I've been dragged into a nightmare I can't wake up from.

And then, the doors at the far end of the court creak open again.

Two figures are shoved into the room, their hands bound in shimmering restraints similar to mine. My breath catches in my throat, my mind racing to process what I'm seeing. It's them. *My parents.*

"Mom? Dad?" Neville's voice is barely above a whisper, trembling with disbelief. His eyes are wide, his usual stoic mask shattered as he stares at them.

They look different from how I remember—older, more weathered, like the years have been unkind. But it's them. It's really them. My chest tightens, and for a moment, everything else fades away.

"Is it…" My voice cracks, and I can barely get the words out. "Is it really you?"

Their heads snap toward us, and the moment their eyes land on Neville, my mother gasps, tears welling up in her eyes. "Neville?" she breathes, her voice breaking. "How… how is this possible?"

"Alive?" My father's voice is hoarse, his expression one of pure shock. "Neville… you're alive?"

They start forward, but the guards flanking them move quickly, grabbing their arms and holding them back. My mother struggles against their grip, her eyes fixed on Neville as tears stream down her face. My father clenches his fists, his jaw tight as he glares at the guards.

"Let them go!" I shout, my voice shaking with anger. "They're not a threat!"

But my plea falls on deaf ears. The guards remain stoic, their grips unyielding as my parents continue to struggle.

"Enough," the Queen says, her voice cold and commanding. The room falls silent, the weight of her presence suffocating. She turns her sharp gaze to my parents, her violet eyes narrowing. "Well, isn't this a touching reunion?"

Ryker's voice cuts through the tension like a blade. "Why are they here?" His midnight-black eyes burn with fury as he glares at his mother. "What is this, Mother? Another one of your games?"

The Queen's lips curl into a faint smile, but there's no warmth in it. "Oh, Ryker, always so dramatic. Isn't it obvious? They're part of this story too."

"Explain," he growls, his fists clenched at his sides. "Now."

The Queen steps forward, her gaze sweeping over all of us

like we're pieces on a chessboard. "Very well. I suppose it's time you all understood the truth."

The room feels colder as she begins to speak, her voice smooth and measured, carrying the weight of centuries. "Once upon a time, I was nothing—a useless human with no power, no purpose. I was weak, insignificant, trapped in a life that offered me nothing."

Her words send a shiver down my spine, but I don't dare interrupt. I can feel Ryker's tension beside me, the way his body seems to vibrate with barely restrained rage.

"Then," she continues, her tone shifting, "I met him. Evander's father. Your stepfather, Ryker. The King of Sirens."

My breath catches, and I glance at Ryker, whose expression darkens further. The King of Sirens? My mind races, trying to piece together what this means, but the Queen doesn't give us time to process.

"He was everything I wasn't," she says, her violet eyes gleaming with something almost nostalgic. "Powerful, commanding, untouchable. He saw potential in me—a weak human who wanted more. And so, I made a choice. I became a vampire."

Her words hang in the air, heavy and suffocating. I can barely breathe, the weight of her story pressing down on me like a physical force.

"I ascended," she says, her voice laced with pride. "I shed my mortal shell and embraced what I was meant to be. And from there, I began building my empire. But there was one loose end—one mistake I needed to correct."

Her gaze shifts to Ryker, and my heart sinks as I see the pain flicker across his face. "You," she says, her tone dripping with disdain. "A human child, weak and useless. A constant reminder of the life I left behind."

"Mother…" Ryker's voice is low, dangerous, but there's an undercurrent of pain that he can't hide.

She ignores him, continuing with her story. "I raised you quietly, biding my time, planning for myself. And when the opportunity came to rid myself of you, I took it. With Evander's help, of course."

My stomach churns, the pieces of the puzzle clicking into place with horrifying clarity. "The Silver Circle," I whisper, the words tasting bitter on my tongue.

The Queen smirks, her gaze flicking to me. "Clever girl. Yes, the Silver Circle. A convenient prison for someone like Ryker. And with him out of the way, I was free to focus on my goals."

I glance at Ryker, whose jaw is tight, his midnight-black eyes blazing with fury and something deeper—betrayal, heartbreak. My chest aches at the sight of him, the weight of everything he's endured crashing over me.

"You used me," he says, his voice trembling with anger. "You threw me away like I was nothing."

"You were nothing," she says coldly. "But look at you now, Ryker. You've survived, grown stronger. Perhaps I underestimated you after all."

Before he can respond, Evander steps forward, his smirk widening. "This is all very touching, but I believe we have more important matters to discuss."

"Evander," Neville growls, his voice laced with fury. "What are you doing here?"

Evander's sea-green eyes gleam with malice as he looks at Neville. "I'm right where I'm supposed to be, little Ashworth. And so are you."

My fists clench at my sides, the mystic chains biting into my skin as I glare at him. "You're a coward," I spit. "Hiding behind your mother, your schemes. You've always been a coward."

His smirk falters, just for a moment, and I feel a small flicker of satisfaction. But the Queen's voice cuts through the tension, sharp and commanding.

"Enough," she says, her gaze sweeping over all of us. "There's more to this story, and you will hear it. But for now, you will stay where you are. Guards."

The guards step forward, grabbing my parents and pulling them back toward the far wall. My mother struggles, her tear-streaked face twisted with desperation as she looks at Neville. "We love you," she says, her voice breaking. "No matter what happens, we love you both."

Her words hit me like a punch to the gut, and I feel the tears welling up in my eyes. I don't know how to respond, don't know how to process any of this. Everything is falling apart, and I feel like I'm drowning.

The Queen turns back to us, her violet eyes gleaming with cold satisfaction. "Now," she says, her voice a silken blade, "shall we begin?"

# 30

# Secrets unveiled

The weight of the mystic chains burns against my wrists as I stand in the center of the Queen's court. The oppressive atmosphere of this place suffocates me, each breath harder to take than the last. My parents are only a few feet away, but it feels like a chasm separates us. Their faces are pale, etched with guilt, and I can't tell if I want to scream at them or demand answers.

When the Queen's voice cuts through the silence, it feels like a blade. "Tell them," she commands, her violet eyes narrowing on my parents. "Tell them what you've been hiding all these years."

My father flinches, his jaw tightening, while my mother looks like she's on the verge of breaking down entirely. She glances at Neville, her gaze lingering for a second too long, and I follow it. My heart twists in my chest when I see him. His shoulders are tense, his head slightly bowed, and his lips pressed into a thin line.

He knows. The realization slams into me like a physical blow, and suddenly, my breathing is uneven. My twin—my own brother—knew whatever secret they've been hiding, and he didn't tell me.

"You knew," I say, the words leaving my mouth before I can stop them. Neville's head snaps up, his eyes meeting mine for the briefest second before flickering away. "Didn't you?" My voice is sharper now, rising in volume. "You knew all along, didn't you?"

"Asterine, I—" Neville starts, but his hesitation only fuels the fire raging inside me.

"You knew," I repeat, my voice shaking with fury. "You knew, and you said nothing."

"It wasn't my place," he says, his tone low, his words clipped.

"Not your place?" I take a step toward him, the chains around my wrists clinking loudly. "I'm your sister, Neville! You had every chance to tell me the truth, and you didn't. Why?"

Before Neville can answer, the Queen chuckles, her voice cold and mocking. "How delightfully dramatic," she drawls. "But enough of this sibling squabble. Your parents owe you the truth, Asterine."

I turn back to them, the anger in my chest mingling with a sharp, cutting sense of betrayal. "Then tell me," I demand, my voice cracking. "Tell me what you've been hiding."

My mother looks like she might crumble on the spot, her lips trembling as she opens her mouth to speak. "You're..." She hesitates, her voice barely above a whisper. "You're special, Asterine."

"Special?" I laugh bitterly, the sound sharp and hollow in the echoing chamber. "What does that even mean?"

"You're the most powerful siphoner born in centuries," my father says, his voice steadier but no less burdened.

The words hang in the air like a death sentence. For

a moment, I forget how to breathe. The most powerful siphoner? In centuries? My vision blurs as I try to comprehend what that means, but the ground beneath my feet feels like it's crumbling.

"You're lying," I say, my voice shaking. "This can't be true."

"It is," my mother says, stepping forward slightly. Tears streak down her face as she continues. "The moment you and Neville were born, we were visited by… her."

"Who?" I ask, my voice cracking.

"The most ancient witch," she says, her tone reverent and fearful. "She told us what you were destined to become—that your power would surpass anything this world has ever known."

I shake my head, taking a shaky step back. "You're saying this ancient witch just showed up at our house and told you I was… what? Some kind of supernatural savior?"

"No," my father interjects. "She told us your power would make you a target. That others would seek to control you. To use you. And that we had to keep you hidden."

"Hidden?" The bitterness seeps into my voice. "You mean lying to me. Pretending I was normal when I wasn't."

"We were trying to protect you," my mother says, her voice breaking. "We didn't know—"

"You didn't know anything," I snap, cutting her off. My hands curl into fists, the chains biting into my skin as the anger rises. "You didn't know what you were doing. You didn't know what I needed. All you cared about was your secrets."

Neville flinches at my words, but I can't stop. "And you," I say, turning to him. "You knew. How long? Weeks? Months?"

"Years," he says softly, his voice barely audible.

The betrayal hits like a physical blow. I stumble back a step, shaking my head. "You knew for years, and you didn't tell me?"

"I thought it was safer," Neville says, his voice trembling. "Safer for everyone."

I laugh bitterly, the sound laced with anger. "And look where that got us."

"Touching," the Queen interjects, her voice dripping with mockery. "But this isn't about your family drama, Asterine. It's about what you are."

I glare at her, my fists clenching tighter. "What do you want from me?"

Her smirk widens, her violet eyes gleaming with malice. "I want your power," she says simply.

"What?" My voice falters, the word barely leaving my lips.

"I've spent centuries building my strength, expanding my reach," she says, her tone cold and commanding. "But even I have limits. You, on the other hand—you're limitless."

I shake my head, my stomach twisting. "You can't take my power. That's not how it works."

Her smile sharpens, sending a chill down my spine. "With the right witches and the right rituals, I can do more than take your power. I can merge with you. Become you."

The room spins around me, the weight of her words crushing. "You're insane," I whisper, my voice trembling. "You'll never get away with this."

The Queen laughs, the sound echoing like shattered glass. "Oh, darling," she says, her voice sickeningly sweet. "I already have."

# 31

# Shattered

I don't even notice the guards moving me back to my cell. My body feels like it's moving on its own, dragged along by their rough hands, but my mind is elsewhere—stuck in the storm of everything that's just happened. The chains bite into my wrists, their cold weight a stark reminder of my vulnerability, but even that pain feels distant.

My parents lied to me.

Neville lied to me.

They've all known what I was, what I could become, and they never told me. They watched me live my life in ignorance, pretending to be normal, while the truth sat in the shadows, waiting to destroy me.

My head throbs, each new thought a sharper dagger than the last. The Queen's voice echoes in my mind, her words wrapping around me like a vice. The most powerful siphoner born in centuries. You're the key to everything. I want to scream, to cry, to break something, but instead, I sit here, trapped in the prison of my own mind.

How could they do this to me? My parents—my own flesh

and blood—they were supposed to protect me. Instead, they lied to me. They kept me blind to who I really am, leaving me to figure it out in the worst way possible. And Neville… my twin. The one person I thought I could trust unconditionally. He knew. For years, he knew.

The betrayal stings more than I can put into words. Neville, my other half, the person who was supposed to understand me better than anyone, kept this massive secret from me. And for what? To protect me? That's what they keep saying—that they were trying to keep me safe. But safe from what? The Queen? The world?  Or was it safer for them, knowing I wouldn't question my place in their carefully crafted lies?

I press my hands to my face, the mystic chains rattling against each other. The cold metal feels suffocating, a cruel parallel to the crushing weight of the truth. What am I supposed to do with this?

I think of the Queen's plan—her desire to merge with me, to take my power and make it her own. The idea of her invading my body, stealing my essence, makes my stomach churn. But what terrifies me even more is how powerless I feel. For the first time in my life, I don't know who I am, and I don't know what to do.

The memories of Evander resurface, uninvited and sharp. I see his face in my mind, that charming smile, those piercing green eyes that once made me believe in something real.  I thought he loved me. I thought what we had was special. But it was all a lie.  Every word, every touch, every moment—it was all part of the Queen's plan.

My throat tightens, a sob threatening to escape, but I bite it back. I can't cry. Not here. Not now.

Evander's betrayal feels like a wound that will never heal.

He made me believe in him, made me trust him, and then he shattered me without a second thought. And now, knowing that he was acting on the Queen's orders only twists the knife deeper. Was anything about us real? Or was I just another pawn in her game?

And then there's Ryker. His silence in the Queen's court, the way he looked at her when she revealed the truth about their connection—it was like watching him break from the inside out. His mother. The Queen. How could someone so cruel, so heartless, have raised him?

I close my eyes, trying to push the image of his face from my mind, but it lingers, stubborn and persistent. Ryker has his own demons, his own pain, and I don't know how to help him when I can't even make sense of my own.

And Eira. Sweet, strong Eira, who has been thrust into this nightmare because of me. She's learning to adapt, finding her way through the chaos, but what if she hadn't survived? What if that rogue vampire had taken her from us?

The guilt claws at my chest, sharp and relentless. Everything feels like my fault. If I hadn't gone to the library that night, if I hadn't been so reckless, none of this would have happened. Eira wouldn't be a vampire. Neville wouldn't be trapped here. And my parents—would they still be free, or would the Queen have found another way to drag them into this?

I take a shaky breath, my eyes flickering to the dim, flickering light outside my cell. The shadows stretch long and thin, crawling up the walls like specters. The silence is deafening, broken only by the faint drip of water somewhere in the distance.

What am I supposed to do now? How am I supposed to move forward when everything I thought I knew has been ripped away?

The Queen's voice echoes in my mind again. You're the key to everything. I hate how her words make me feel. She's wrong—I'm not a key. I'm not a weapon or a prize to be claimed. But even as I think it, a small voice in the back of my mind whispers: What if she's right? What if I am something more?

The thought terrifies me. If I truly am the most powerful siphoner born in centuries, what does that mean? What am I capable of? And if my parents were so afraid of my power that they hid it from me, what happens if I lose control?

I wrap my arms around myself, the chains rattling as I try to steady my breathing. I can't afford to break. Not now. Not when so many people are counting on me.

But it's hard. It's so damn hard.

The minutes stretch into hours, or maybe it's only seconds. Time feels meaningless in this place, the walls pressing in on me, the darkness growing heavier with every passing moment. My thoughts swirl like a storm, each one darker and more chaotic than the last.

I think of my parents, their tearful faces etched with guilt. They kept me in the dark for my whole life, and now they expect me to understand. To forgive. But how can I? How do I reconcile the people who raised me with the ones who lied to me?

I think of Neville, my twin, my other half. He's always been my anchor, the one constant in my life. And yet, he kept this from me too. How do I trust him now, when he's been keeping such a monumental secret for so long?

And then there's me. Asterine Ashworth. The most powerful siphoner born in centuries. The girl who has no idea who she really is.

I close my eyes, the tears finally spilling over as I bury my face in my hands. I'm angry. I'm scared. And most of all, I'm lost.

But even in the chaos, a small spark of determination flares to life in my chest. I don't know what's coming, and I don't know if I can face it. But I have to. For Eira. For Neville. For myself.

Because no matter what the Queen says, my power is mine. And I'm not going to let her take it from me.

# 32

# Breaking point

The grating sound of the cell door slamming shut echoes through the dim chamber, making me flinch. I press myself against the cold stone wall, my knees drawn to my chest as I try to make sense of what's happening. The mystic chains are still wrapped tightly around my wrists, their draining weight making every movement feel impossible.

And then I hear them.

"Asterine?" Neville's voice is the first to cut through the suffocating silence, hesitant and searching. My head snaps up, and I see the guards shoving him, Eira, Ryker, and my parents into the same cramped cell. My stomach twists at the sight of them, but I don't move. I can't.

The guards lock the door behind them and leave without a word, their heavy boots echoing down the corridor until the sound fades completely. The silence that follows is deafening, broken only by the rattling of chains and the faint, shallow breaths of everyone in the room.

"Asterine..." Neville tries again, stepping toward me, but I shrink back instinctively, my heart pounding in my chest.

"Don't," I say, my voice hoarse and trembling. "Don't come near me."

He freezes, his face falling as he looks at me. "Asterine, please. I—"

"You knew," I snap, cutting him off. The words spill out of me like venom, my anger bubbling to the surface. "You knew what I was, what she wanted, and you didn't say a damn thing."

"I was trying to protect you!" Neville shouts, his voice breaking. "Do you think I wanted this to happen?"

"Protect me?" I laugh bitterly, the sound sharp and hollow. "You call lying to me protection? Keeping me in the dark while everyone else knew the truth?"

"Not everyone knew," Ryker says from the corner of the cell, his voice low but laced with frustration. "Some of us were just as blindsided as you."

"Oh, don't even start," I snap, my eyes narrowing on him. "You've been lying to me too, Ryker. About your mother, about everything. So don't act like you're innocent in all of this."

Ryker's jaw tightens, his midnight-black eyes glinting with barely restrained anger. "You think I wanted any of this? You think I wanted her to be my mother? To find out everything I've ever known was a lie?"

"Enough!" my father's voice booms, silencing the room. He steps forward, his face a mask of anger and guilt. "We don't have time for this. We need to figure out a way out of here."

"A way out?" I repeat, incredulous. "You're the reason we're in this mess! If you had just told me the truth—"

"We were trying to protect you!" my mother cuts in, her voice trembling with emotion. "You don't understand, Asterine. You were born with a gift—a power so great it could destroy you if you weren't careful."

"And you thought the best way to handle that was to hide it from me?" I shoot back. "To let me stumble around in the dark while everyone else made decisions for me?"

"We didn't have a choice!" my father shouts, his voice cracking. "The Queen would have found you sooner if we hadn't kept you hidden. We were trying to keep you safe."

"Safe?" I laugh again, the sound bitter and full of pain. "Do I look safe to you? We're all trapped here because of your lies. Because of your cowardice."

The room falls silent for a moment, the weight of my words pressing down on all of us. I can feel the tension thick in the air, the anger and guilt radiating from everyone around me.

And then Eira speaks, her voice quiet but steady. "Enough, all of you."

We all turn to her, surprised by the calm authority in her tone. She stands near the back of the cell, her pale face framed by the dim light filtering through the bars. "Arguing isn't going to get us anywhere. We're in this together, whether we like it or not."

"Together?" I repeat, shaking my head. "That's easy for you to say, Eira. You weren't the one everyone lied to."

"No, but I am the one who got dragged into this because of you," she says, her words sharp but not unkind. "I didn't ask for any of this, Asterine. None of us did. But here we are."

Her words hit harder than I expect, and for a moment, I can't speak. She's right, of course. None of us chose this. None of us wanted this. But that doesn't make the betrayal sting any less.

"She's right," Ryker says, his voice softer now. "Fighting each other isn't going to help. We need to focus on how to stop my mother and get out of here."

"And how exactly do we do that?" Neville asks, his tone laced with frustration. "We're chained up, powerless, and surrounded by her guards."

Ryker's jaw tightens, his eyes narrowing as he stares at the ground. "I don't know. But we'll figure something out. We always do."

Silence falls over the group again, the weight of our situation pressing down on all of us. I lean back against the wall, my head resting against the cold stone as I close my eyes. My mind is racing, the anger and fear swirling together in a storm I can't control.

"Why didn't you tell me?" I ask softly, my voice trembling. I don't open my eyes, but I know Neville is looking at me. "You had so many chances. So many opportunities to tell me the truth. Why didn't you?"

"Because I was afraid," he admits, his voice barely above a whisper. "Afraid of what would happen if you found out. Afraid of what you would become."

His words hit like a punch to the gut, and I feel my chest tighten. "You were afraid of me?"

"I wasn't afraid of you," he says quickly. "I was afraid for you. You don't understand how powerful you are, Asterine. How dangerous that power can be."

I open my eyes, staring at him through the dim light. "Maybe if you had told me, I would have understood. Maybe if you had trusted me, I wouldn't feel so alone right now."

Neville flinches, his shoulders sagging as the guilt washes over him. "I'm sorry," he says, his voice breaking. "I thought I was doing the right thing."

The silence that follows is heavy, but this time, it's less charged. The anger still simmers beneath the surface, but it's mixed with something else—regret, maybe, or understanding.

I don't know what's going to happen next. I don't know how we're going to get out of this or if we even can. But for now, we're all we have. And for better or worse, we're in this together.

# 33

# The Merger

The guards come for us just as the first rays of dawn begin to seep through the cracks in the stone walls of our cell. My stomach churns as I'm yanked roughly to my feet, the cold bite of the mystic chains around my wrists making me shiver. The air feels heavier than usual, thick with an ominous energy that makes my skin crawl.

"Asterine!" Neville's voice is urgent, but there's nothing he can do as the guards shove him forward, forcing all of us into a single line. Ryker growls low in his throat, his midnight-black eyes darting around the corridor, searching for an opening, a weakness—anything. Eira is quieter, her face pale but her jaw clenched with determination. My parents walk silently, their faces lined with guilt and fear.

We're led through the twisting corridors of the Queen's domain, the walls pressing in around us like a living thing. The sound of our chains echoes in the silence, a grim reminder of how powerless we are. My heart pounds in my chest, each beat a drumroll leading to the unknown. This is it. Whatever the Queen has planned, it's happening now.

When we're finally brought into the room, I can't help but gasp. It's massive, the ceiling arching high above us, painted with dark, swirling patterns that seem to move if you look at them too long. The air is thick with the scent of herbs and smoke, and a circle of witches stands in the center, their faces obscured by dark hoods. At the far end of the room, the Queen sits on a throne carved from black stone, her violet eyes gleaming with anticipation.

"Welcome," she says, her voice smooth and chilling. "It's time."

The guards shove us forward, forcing us into the center of the room. The witches begin to chant, their voices low and guttural, sending a shiver down my spine. The runes carved into the floor begin to glow, their light pulsing in time with the chanting.

I can feel the energy in the room shifting, pressing down on me like a physical weight. My chest tightens, and I struggle to breathe as the realization hits me: This is the ritual. This is how she's going to take my power.

"Stop!" Ryker's voice cuts through the chanting, sharp and commanding. He steps forward despite the chains, his midnight-black eyes blazing with fury. "Mother, this is madness. You can't do this."

The Queen's smile widens, her gaze cool and unyielding. "Oh, but I can, my dear. And I will."

Before Ryker can respond, one of the witches steps forward, holding a dagger made of shimmering, iridescent metal. My stomach churns as I recognize it—mystic metal, designed to drain and bind magical energy.

"No!" Neville shouts, struggling against the guards holding him. "You can't do this to her!"

The Queen raises an eyebrow, her expression almost bored. "Oh, I can't? Watch me."

The witch approaches me, the dagger glinting in the dim light. My heart pounds as I try to step back, but the guards hold me firmly in place. The blade is so close now, the runes etched into its surface glowing faintly. I can feel its pull, its hunger for my power, and I know that if it touches me, it will be over.

And then, chaos erupts.

The door at the far end of the room bursts open with a deafening crash, and three figures step through the smoke and debris. My breath catches in my throat as I recognize them: Maeve, Fabian, and Jocosa.

"What the—" one of the guards starts, but he doesn't get to finish. Maeve lunges forward, her movements impossibly fast, and before my eyes, her body begins to shift. Her clothes rip as her limbs elongate, her face contorting into something feral and terrifying. In seconds, she's no longer Maeve—she's a werewolf?, her golden fur glinting in the dim light, her eyes blazing with fury. She has been a werewolf? This entire time? Damn; another secret.

Fabian isn't far behind. His transformation is just as horrifying, his once-charming features replaced by a snarling maw and razor-sharp claws.

Why did both of them never reveal it to anyone? They both look so ferocious in this state. I can only imagine them being Maeve and Fabian. I just keep watching in fear and awe at the same time. Both the werewolves look so huge and powerful. I knew werewolves existed; thanks to my library reading habit, but never thought they would look so—werewolf-ish? I'm absolutely dumbfounded.

The room erupts into screams and shouts as the guards try to regroup, but it's too late. The werewolves are already among them, their claws slashing and teeth tearing.

"Werewolves," Ryker breathes, his voice filled with shock. "They're werewolves."

The Queen rises from her throne, her face a mask of rage and disbelief. "Impossible," she hisses. "Kill them!"

The witches scatter, their chants forgotten as the werewolves tear through the guards. Jocosa steps forward, her hands glowing with a faint blue light as she sends a blast of energy toward the nearest witch, knocking them off their feet.

"Get them out of here!" she shouts, her voice ringing through the chaos.

Maeve and Fabian fight like nothing I've ever seen. Their movements are a blur, a deadly combination of speed and strength that leaves the guards scrambling. One of them lunges at Maeve, but she sidesteps effortlessly, her claws raking across his chest. The man crumples to the ground, groaning in pain.

I can barely process what's happening. The room is a whirlwind of noise and movement, the smell of blood and smoke filling the air. My heart races as I look around, searching for an opening, a way to escape.

"Asterine!" Neville's voice snaps me back to reality. He's beside me now, his chains broken, his face set with determination. "We need to move!"

"But the Queen—"

"We'll deal with her later," he says firmly. "Right now, we need to survive."

I nod, my legs shaking as I take a step forward. My chains feel heavier than ever, the weight of the mystic metal dragging me down, but I force myself to keep moving. Jocosa appears at my side, her hands glowing as she focuses on the chains.

"This might sting," she warns, and before I can respond, a burst of energy surges through me. The chains shatter, and I stumble forward, gasping as the weight is lifted.

"Thanks," I manage to say, but she's already moving, her focus shifting to Eira.

The Queen's voice cuts through the chaos, sharp and commanding. "Enough!" Her presence fills the room, her violet eyes blazing as she steps forward. "You think this changes anything? You think a couple of mutts and a wannabe witch can stop me?"

Maeve growls, her golden fur bristling as she turns to face the Queen. Fabian steps up beside her, his eyes locked on the enemy. "We're not done yet," he snarls, his voice a low, guttural growl.

The Queen smirks, her gaze flicking between them. "Do you know what happens to vampires when they're bitten by werewolves?" she asks, her tone almost conversational. "It's fatal. A slow, painful death. Do you really think I'll let you get close enough to try?"

The room goes still for a moment, the tension so thick it's almost suffocating. And then, with a roar, Maeve and Fabian charge.

# 34

# Werewolves and Vampires can never be friends

The room is a whirlwind of chaos—growls, shouts, and the deafening clash of magic and claws. Maeve and Fabian fight like predators born for the hunt, their werewolf forms a blur of deadly motion. Jocosa, her hands glowing with flickering blue energy, is already moving toward me and Neville, her sharp gaze darting to the guards surrounding us.

"Stay close to me," she orders, her voice firm but not unkind.

Neville and I nod, our eyes locked on her as she raises her hands. A pulse of energy radiates from her fingertips, slamming into the guards with a force that sends them sprawling. The air crackles with power, and for the first time since being dragged into this nightmare, hope flares in my chest.

"Jocosa, what are you—?" I begin, but she cuts me off.

"We're leaving. Now."

The Queen's enraged scream cuts through the din, her violet eyes blazing as she strides toward us. "You think you can escape me? You think you can run?"

"Watch me," Jocosa snaps, her hands moving in a blur of motion as she begins chanting under her breath.

The air around us shifts, the temperature dropping as the glow of her magic intensifies. The runes carved into the stone walls flicker ominously, as if reacting to the surge of power. I feel the ground tremble beneath my feet, and then, with a deafening crack, a portal begins to form in the air before us.

It's unlike anything I've ever seen—a swirling vortex of light and shadow, its edges crackling with raw energy. The sight of it sends a shiver down my spine, but Jocosa doesn't hesitate.

"Move!" she shouts, motioning for us to follow her.

Neville grabs my arm, pulling me toward the portal. I glance over my shoulder just in time to see Maeve and Fabian break away from their fight, their golden and tawny forms bounding toward us with supernatural speed. Ryker is right behind them, his midnight-black eyes locked on mine as he reaches out, urging me forward.

The Queen screams something unintelligible, her voice thick with fury, but it's too late. One by one, we dive into the portal, the swirling energy swallowing us whole.

The world shifts violently around me, the sensation like being yanked in a dozen different directions at once. My stomach flips, and for a moment, I think I might be sick. But then, just as quickly as it began, the chaos stops.

I stumble forward, falling to my knees on soft, damp earth. The scent of pine and moss fills the air, and when I look up, I realize we're outside. The towering trees of a dense forest rise around us, their branches stretching high into the night sky.

"We made it," Jocosa says, her voice tight with exhaustion.

"Not for long," Ryker growls, his eyes scanning the tree line.

"They'll come after us. We need to move."

He's right. Even as he speaks, the faint sound of shouting reaches my ears, carried on the wind. The Queen's army is coming.

"Let's go!" Neville says, pulling me to my feet. "We have to keep moving."

We take off, the forest floor crunching beneath our feet as we run. The darkness presses in around us, the faint moonlight barely enough to guide our way. My heart pounds in my chest, my breath coming in ragged gasps as adrenaline propels me forward.

Behind me, Maeve and Fabian move like shadows, their werewolf forms gliding effortlessly through the trees. Eira is close by, her pale face set with determination despite the fear flickering in her eyes. Jocosa is ahead, her glowing hands lighting the way as she leads us deeper into the forest.

But it's Ryker who stays closest to me, his presence a steady anchor in the chaos. I can feel his eyes on me, watching my every move, ready to catch me if I stumble.

The sound of pursuit grows louder, the Queen's army crashing through the underbrush in the distance. My stomach twists with fear, but I force myself to focus on the path ahead. We have to keep going. We can't let them catch us.

Suddenly, Maeve lets out a low growl, her golden fur bristling as she comes to a stop. "They're close," she says, her voice a guttural rumble. "Too close."

"We need a plan," Fabian adds, his tawny form tense and alert.

"We don't have time for a plan," Ryker snaps. "We keep moving."

"No," Jocosa says firmly, turning to face him. "If we keep

running without a plan, they'll surround us. We need to figure out our next move."

Her words make sense, but the rising panic in my chest makes it hard to think. I glance around, my eyes darting to the shadows that seem to press closer with every passing second. "What about the portal?" I ask, my voice trembling. "Can you make another one?"

"Not yet," Jocosa says, her tone apologetic. "The energy it took to create that one… I need time to recover."

Time we don't have.

The sound of the army grows louder, and my heart sinks as I see the first glint of armor through the trees. They're here.

"Split up," Ryker says suddenly, his voice sharp. "We'll regroup later. It's the only way to throw them off."

"Are you insane?" Neville snaps. "We're stronger together."

"We're also easier to catch together," Ryker counters, his midnight-black eyes flashing. "Trust me, Neville. This is the only way."

There's a tense moment of silence, and then, reluctantly, Neville nods. "Fine. But you'd better know what you're doing."

We split into pairs—Neville with Eira, Maeve with Fabian, and me with Ryker. Jocosa stays behind, her glowing hands raised as she begins casting a spell to create a diversion.

"Stay close," Ryker says, his voice low as he takes my arm.

We take off again, the forest a blur around us as we weave through the trees. The sound of the army fades slightly, but it's still there, a constant reminder of how close we are to being caught. My legs ache, my lungs burn, but I don't stop. I can't.

Ryker's grip on my arm is firm but not harsh, his presence a steady reassurance in the chaos. Despite everything, I find myself glancing at him, the determined set of his jaw, the way his copper hair catches the faint light filtering through the trees.

"How do you stay so calm?" I ask, my voice barely audible over the sound of our footsteps.

He glances at me, a faint smirk tugging at his lips. "Practice."

Despite myself, I feel a small flicker of amusement. But it's short-lived as the sound of shouting grows louder again, the Queen's army closing in.

Ryker pulls me to a stop, his eyes scanning the area. "This way," he says, tugging me toward a dense thicket of trees.

We duck into the underbrush, the branches scratching at my skin as we crouch low, trying to stay hidden. My heart pounds in my chest, each beat echoing in my ears like a drum.

The sound of footsteps draws closer, the faint glint of armor visible through the foliage. I hold my breath, every muscle in my body tense as I wait for them to pass.

Please, don't let them find us.

The footsteps pause, and I feel my stomach drop. One of the soldiers is standing just a few feet away, his eyes scanning the area. I can see the glint of his sword, the way his fingers tighten around the hilt as he moves closer.

Beside me, Ryker tenses, his midnight-black eyes narrowing as he prepares to spring into action. My pulse quickens, fear and adrenaline surging through me.

But then, a distant shout draws the soldier's attention. He hesitates for a moment, and then he turns, running toward the sound.

I exhale a shaky breath, relief flooding through me as the footsteps fade.

"We need to keep moving," Ryker whispers, his voice low but urgent.

I nod, my legs trembling as I follow him deeper into the forest. The chase isn't over yet.

# 35

# The Escapade

The sound of the Queen's army grows louder with every passing second. The ground beneath my feet trembles, the vibrations crawling up my legs and settling into my chest like an ominous drumbeat. Jocosa's spell gave us a momentary head start, but now, with no portal left to escape through, we're out of options.

"Stand together," my father says, stepping into the center of the clearing. His voice is calm, but there's a weight to it, a certainty that sends a chill down my spine. "They'll be here any second."

My mother moves to his side, her hands already glowing faintly with magic. It's the first time I've ever seen her use her abilities, and the sight sends a pang of something—anger? awe?—through me. They've spent my entire life hiding what I am, and now, here they are, wielding the very powers they kept from me.

"They're here," Ryker says, his voice low and sharp as his midnight-black eyes scan the tree line.

The first wave of guards bursts through the trees, their armor gleaming in the pale moonlight. They move in formation, their weapons raised, their faces set with grim determination. The sight of them makes my stomach churn, my heart pounding so hard it feels like it might burst from my chest.

And then the fighting begins.

The guards charge, their swords slicing through the air with deadly precision. My father is the first to react, raising his hand and sending a blast of energy toward the oncoming wave. The force of it sends several guards flying backward, their weapons clattering to the ground.

My mother steps forward, her movements fluid and precise as she conjures a wall of fire to block their advance. The flames roar to life, casting flickering shadows across the clearing. "Hold the line!" she shouts, her voice ringing with authority.

Neville moves next, his fists glowing as he siphons energy from the ground beneath him. He channels it into a devastating punch, the shock wave knocking a group of guards off their feet. "Stay together!" he yells, his voice commanding despite the chaos.

Eira is a blur of motion, her vampire speed and strength making her nearly impossible to track. She grabs one guard by the collar, throwing him into a tree with a sickening crunch. Her pale face is fierce, her fangs bared as she snarls at another soldier who tries to approach.

Ryker fights with a precision that's almost beautiful to watch. His copper hair catches the moonlight as he moves, his midnight-black eyes locked onto his enemies. He dodges a sword swing with inhuman speed, retaliating with a blow that sends the guard sprawling.

Jocosa stands at the edge of the clearing, her hands glowing as she conjures barrier after barrier, deflecting arrows and bolts of energy. Her magic is wild but controlled, each spell calculated to protect and defend.

Maeve and Fabian are in their werewolf forms, their growls echoing through the clearing as they tear through the ranks of guards. Maeve's golden fur is streaked with blood, her claws slicing through armor like paper. Fabian's larger frame barrels into the enemy, his snarls sending chills down my spine.

And then there's me—chained, powerless, and utterly useless. I stand frozen at the edge of the chaos, my heart pounding as I watch everyone I care about risk their lives. This is my fault. If I weren't here, if I weren't what they're after, none of this would be happening.

"Move, Asterine!" my father shouts, snapping me out of my daze. A guard charges toward me, his sword raised, and I stumble back, panic flaring in my chest. Before I can react, my mother steps in front of me, her hands glowing as she sends a blast of energy at the guard, knocking him to the ground.

"Stay behind us!" she commands, her tone leaving no room for argument.

The fight rages on, the clearing filled with the sounds of clashing metal, snarls, and the occasional burst of magic. The Queen's army seems endless, their numbers far outweighing ours, but we fight with a ferocity born of desperation.

My father's movements are swift and deliberate, his attacks precise as he takes down guard after guard. My mother is a whirlwind of fire and energy, her magic burning brighter with each spell. Neville fights like a man possessed, his siphoning abilities amplifying his strength and speed.

Eira is relentless, her newfound vampire instincts turning her into a force of nature. Even Jocosa, with her reserves of magic running low, refuses to back down, her hands still glowing faintly as she deflects attack after attack.

But it's Maeve and Fabian who command the battlefield. Their werewolf forms are a blur of motion, their claws and teeth tearing through the enemy with terrifying efficiency. Maeve's golden fur glints in the moonlight, her growls sending chills down my spine.

And then, it happens.

The Queen's guards begin to shift their tactics, focusing their attacks on Maeve and Fabian. They've realized the werewolves are the biggest threat, and they're determined to take them down.

"Maeve, watch out!" I scream as I see a guard lunging toward her, his silver-tipped spear aimed at her chest. She dodges at the last second, her claws raking across his armor, but another guard is already closing in.

Fabian moves to help her, his tawny form colliding with the second guard, but it's too late. A third guard emerges from the shadows, his blade glinting in the moonlight as he drives it into Maeve's side.

"No!" The word tears from my throat as Maeve lets out a strangled yelp, her golden form collapsing to the ground. The guard raises his weapon for another strike, but Fabian is on him in an instant, his claws tearing through the man's armor.

I fall to my knees beside Maeve, my hands trembling as I reach for her. Her golden eyes meet mine, filled with pain and something else—resignation.

"Maeve," I whisper, my voice breaking. "No, no, no. You're going to be okay. We'll get you out of here."

She tries to smile, but it comes out as a grimace. "Asterine," she says, her voice weak. "You have to… you have to fight. Don't… don't let them win."

Her body shudders, her golden fur fading as she shifts back into her human form. Blood pools beneath her, staining the earth a deep crimson.

"No!" Fabian's roar echoes through the clearing as he cradles Maeve's lifeless body, his tawny fur slick with her blood. His grief is raw, a guttural sound that cuts through the chaos like a knife.

The rest of the group freezes, their faces pale as they take in the scene. Even the guards seem momentarily stunned, their movements faltering.

"She's gone," Jocosa says softly, her voice trembling as tears stream down her face.

# 36

## The Cost of Survival

Maeve's golden eyes stare lifelessly at the sky, her body sprawled on the forest floor. Blood seeps from the gaping wound at her side, darkening the earth beneath her. Fabian clutches her, his guttural howls piercing through the chaos around us. The sound slices through me like a blade, sharp and relentless.

Time seems to stop. The clashing swords, the howls of the guards, even the bursts of magic from my companions—all of it fades into a dull hum as the reality of Maeve's death crashes over me.

I can't breathe. My chest tightens, my lungs refusing to fill with air. Maeve's gone.

The guilt comes first, sharp and unforgiving. I should have done something. I should have helped her. Why didn't I do anything?

Then comes the anger.

It starts as a flicker, a small flame that quickly grows into a roaring inferno. My hands clench into fists, my nails digging into my palms as I force myself to stand. My legs shake beneath me, but I don't care.

And then I see her.

The Queen.

Valora stands at the edge of the battlefield, her violet eyes gleaming with a cold, detached amusement. She doesn't move, doesn't lift a finger to join the fight. She just watches, like a puppet master admiring her handiwork.

The fire inside me roars, consuming every other thought. This is her fault. She did this. She brought us here. She sent her guards. She killed Maeve.

I barely register the weight of the chains around my wrists as I start moving toward her.

"Asterine, stop!" Neville's voice is sharp and commanding, but I don't listen.

He grabs my arm, his grip firm and unrelenting. "What are you doing?"

"I'm ending this," I snap, pulling my arm free.

His eyes widen, his face pale with alarm. "You can't! You don't know what you're doing—"

"I don't care!" My voice trembles, but the conviction in it is unyielding. "She killed Maeve. She brought us here. She—she doesn't get to walk away from this."

Neville opens his mouth to argue, but Ryker steps forward, his midnight-black eyes locking onto mine. "Let her go," he says quietly, his voice steady.

"What?" Neville's head snaps toward him, disbelief written all over his face.

"She's right," Ryker says, his gaze unwavering. "This ends now."

For a moment, Neville looks like he's about to protest, but then his shoulders sag, and he steps back.

"Asterine," he says softly, his voice trembling. "Be careful."

I don't respond. I can't. My focus is singular, fixed entirely on Valora.

The forest feels colder as I approach her, the damp air clinging to my skin. Each step feels heavier than the last, my heart pounding so hard it drowns out the chaos behind me.

Valora's back is to me as I close the distance between us, her dark cloak billowing slightly in the breeze. The moonlight catches on her silver hair, turning it into a glowing halo that seems almost too human for the monster she is.

She doesn't see me coming.

I reach out, my fingers brushing against the fabric of her cloak. The moment I make contact, a surge of energy slams into me, so powerful it nearly knocks me off my feet.

Valora spins around, her violet eyes widening in surprise. "You," she hisses, her voice dripping with venom.

Before she can react, I grab her arm, the chains on my wrists clinking faintly as I latch onto her. The connection snaps into place, and I feel it instantly—the raw, untamed power that flows through her veins.

It's overwhelming. Her magic is like a tidal wave, crashing into me with a force that steals my breath. My knees buckle, but I hold on, siphoning the energy with everything I have.

Valora screams, the sound piercing and inhuman. She claws at my hands, trying to break free, but I don't let go. Her magic is wild and chaotic, thrumming with a life of its own as it pours into me.

My vision blurs, the edges of the world fading as the power takes over. It feels like fire, searing and unrelenting, coursing through every vein in my body. My chest heaves as I struggle to contain it, to control it.

Valora's struggles grow weaker, her body convulsing as I drain her magic. The glow in her violet eyes dims, her strength ebbing away until she collapses to the ground.

When it's over, she lies motionless, her once-commanding presence reduced to a fragile, unconscious shell.

I stumble back, my chest heaving as I clutch at my wrists. The mystic chains feel heavier now, their cold weight biting into my skin. My body trembles, every nerve on fire from the power I've taken.

"Asterine!" Neville's voice is frantic as he runs toward me. "What did you do?"

"I—I don't know," I whisper, my voice shaky.

The others gather around, their faces pale with shock. Jocosa's glowing hands hover near me, her eyes scanning my face with a mix of awe and fear.

"She drained her," Ryker says, his voice low and disbelieving.

The magic inside me is too much. It burns, searing through my veins like molten lava. I clench my fists, my nails digging into my palms as I try to hold it in.

"Asterine," Neville says, his voice softer now, almost pleading. "You can't contain that much power. You have to release it."

"How?" I choke out, tears streaming down my face.

"You've done it before," he says. "You just have to focus. Let it go."

My heart races, the weight of his words pressing down on me. The power thrums inside me, alive and relentless, begging to be unleashed.

"Everyone," I manage to say, my voice trembling. "Get behind me. Now."

They hesitate for a moment, their fear palpable. But then Ryker steps forward, his midnight-black eyes locking onto mine. "Do it," he says simply.

One by one, they move behind me, their movements cautious and hesitant. Even my parents step back, their gazes heavy with guilt and fear.

I close my eyes, my hands trembling as I stretch them out in front of me. The magic is wild, thrashing inside me like a caged beast. I take a deep breath, focusing on the energy, trying to shape it, control it.

And then, I let it go.

The release is explosive. A blinding light engulfs the clearing, the ground trembling as a wave of energy radiates outward. The air crackles with electricity, the force of the magic sending shock waves through the forest.

The Queen's guards don't stand a chance. One by one, they disintegrate, their bodies turning to Asterine that scatters in the wind. Their screams are cut short, the sheer power of the magic consuming them completely.

The trees tremble, their branches swaying violently as the shock waves ripple through the clearing. Even the ground beneath me feels unstable, the raw energy reshaping the earth itself.

When it's over, the clearing is silent. The guards are gone, reduced to nothing more than dust.

The remaining reinforcements freeze, their faces pale with terror as they stare at me. For a moment, no one moves. And then, as if a signal has been given, they turn and flee, their footsteps echoing in the stillness as they carry Valora's unconscious body away.

I collapse to the ground, my body trembling with exhaustion. The power is gone now, drained completely, but the weight of what I've done lingers.

"Asterine!" Neville is at my side in an instant, his hands gripping my shoulders. "Are you okay?"

"I don't know," I whisper, my voice barely audible.

The others gather around, their faces etched with a mix of relief and shock. Ryker kneels beside me, his copper hair disheveled, his midnight-black eyes scanning my face.

"That was..." He trails off, shaking his head. "I don't even know what that was."

"It was reckless," my mother says, her tone sharp despite the tears in her eyes.

"But she saved us," Jocosa says softly, her gaze flicking to the now-empty clearing.

I close my eyes, exhaustion washing over me like a tidal wave. The battle is over, but the cost of survival is one we'll carry forever.

# 37

# The Way Home

The clearing feels hollow now, a vacuum where life and hope have been sucked out. The ashes of the Queen's guards drift in the wind, scattered like haunting remnants of the chaos that unfolded moments ago. Despite the victory—if we can even call it that—every breath feels heavier, every sound muted.

My gaze drifts to Fabian, who still cradles Maeve's lifeless body in his arms. His tawny hair is matted with blood, his face etched with a grief so raw it makes my chest ache. He hasn't spoken since her final breath, hasn't moved from the spot where he fell to his knees.

I want to say something—anything—but the words refuse to come. What can I possibly say that wouldn't sound hollow? That wouldn't feel like an insult to the enormity of his pain?

The others are quiet too, their faces pale and drawn. Jocosa stands a few feet away, her hands glowing faintly as she examines the clearing with a furrowed brow. She's already working, her mind racing for a way to get us out of here.

"We need to go," Ryker says finally, his voice breaking the

oppressive silence. His midnight-black eyes scan the tree line, sharp and alert. "The Queen's army might be scattered, but they'll regroup. We can't stay here."

Fabian doesn't react, his gaze fixed on Maeve's face. Jocosa steps forward, hesitating for a moment before placing a gentle hand on his shoulder.

"Fabian," she says softly, her voice trembling. "We have to move. Maeve wouldn't want us to stay here and risk everything."

For a moment, he doesn't respond. Then, slowly, he nods, his movements stiff and mechanical. He stands, cradling Maeve's body as if she might shatter if he lets go.

I swallow hard, my throat tight. The sight of him like this—broken and silent—is almost too much to bear. This shouldn't have happened. She shouldn't be gone.

Jocosa turns to Neville and his parents, her expression determined. "I can open a portal," she says, her voice steady despite the exhaustion evident in her every word. "But I'll need your help. The energy it'll take… I can't do it alone."

Neville nods without hesitation, stepping forward. "Tell me what to do."

His parents exchange a glance, their faces shadowed with worry, but they nod as well. My father steps closer, his hand resting briefly on Neville's shoulder. "We'll help."

I watch them move into position, their movements precise and practiced. How long have they been using their powers? How long have they been hiding this part of themselves from me? The questions swirl in my mind, bitter and relentless, but I push them aside. There's no time for anger. Not now.

Ryker steps closer to me, his presence a steadying force in the chaos. "Are you okay?" he asks quietly, his copper hair catching the faint moonlight.

I shake my head. "No. But I don't think anyone is."

He doesn't say anything, just nods, his midnight-black eyes flicking to the others as they begin their work.

Jocosa raises her hands, the glow around them intensifying as she begins to chant under her breath. The words are foreign, their cadence rhythmic and haunting. Neville and his parents mirror her movements, their own hands glowing faintly as they channel their energy into the spell.

The air around us shifts, growing colder. The ground trembles faintly, the vibrations crawling up my legs. I take a step back, my gaze locked on the swirling energy forming in the center of the clearing.

It starts as a faint shimmer, like heat waves rising from the earth. Then it grows, expanding into a swirling vortex of light and shadow. The edges crackle with raw energy, the air humming with power.

Jocosa's voice rises, her chanting growing louder and more forceful. Sweat beads on her forehead, her expression tight with concentration. Neville's face is pale, his jaw clenched as he channels his power into the spell.

My parents stand on either side of him, their hands glowing as they lend their strength to the portal. Seeing them like this—united, powerful—stirs something inside me. They've been hiding so much. How much more is there that I don't know?

The portal stabilizes, its swirling energy casting an eerie glow over the clearing. Jocosa lowers her hands, swaying slightly as the strain catches up with her. Ryker is by her side in an instant, steadying her with a firm hand on her arm.

"It's ready," she says, her voice barely above a whisper.

Fabian steps forward first, Maeve's body cradled in his arms.

His movements are slow, almost reverent, as he approaches the portal. The sight of him carrying her like that—so careful, so protective—makes my chest ache all over again.

The others follow, moving through the portal one by one. Neville hesitates at the edge, his gaze flicking back to me. "Asterine, come on."

I nod, forcing my legs to move. The energy of the portal crackles against my skin as I step through, the world blurring and twisting around me.

When we emerge on the other side, the familiar sight of Harlow Academy greets us. The towering Gothic buildings rise against the night sky, their spires silhouetted by the faint glow of the moon.

The courtyard is silent, the air still and heavy. It feels like a lifetime since I last stood here, though it's only been days.

Fabian doesn't stop, his steps unsteady but determined as he carries Maeve toward the main building. The rest of us follow in silence, the weight of everything we've lost hanging heavy in the air.

I can't stop thinking about her.

Maeve.

Her laughter, her sharp wit, the way she always made everything feel a little less overwhelming. She's gone, and there's nothing we can do to change that.

If I'd been stronger, faster, better… maybe she wouldn't have died. Maybe she'd still be here, teasing Fabian or arguing with Jocosa.

My hands tremble at my sides, the chains around my wrists a constant reminder of my failure. I should have done more. I should have been better.

We gather in the common room, the silence oppressive.

Fabian sits in the corner, Maeve's body wrapped gently in a blanket beside him. His tawny hair hangs in his face, his shoulders slumped in a way that makes him look smaller, diminished.

Jocosa is seated beside him, her glowing hands dim now, her expression unreadable. Ryker stands near the window, his midnight-black eyes scanning the courtyard below. Eira and Neville sit together, their hands clasped tightly, their faces pale and drawn.

No one speaks.

The weight of what we've lost hangs heavy in the air, pressing down on all of us. The victory feels hollow, the cost too great.

As I sit there, my gaze drifting to the window, a thought takes root in my mind.

This isn't over.

The Queen might be weakened, her army scattered, but she's not gone. And until she is, none of us are safe.

Maeve's death won't be in vain.

I'll make sure of it.

# 38

# Justifications

The morning light creeps through the Gothic windows of the common room, casting long shadows on the stone walls. The weight of everything we've endured presses down on me like a physical force, suffocating and inescapable. Fabian sits silently in the corner, his head bowed as he clutches Maeve's blanket-wrapped body. The rest of us are scattered across the room, too drained to speak, too shattered to move.

I sit by the window, staring out at the courtyard below. The faint murmur of the students' morning routines filters through the glass, a stark contrast to the chaos still raging inside me.

Maeve's laughter echoes in my mind, unbidden and relentless. I can see her sharp grin, hear her sarcastic quips, feel the warmth of her presence—and then it's gone, ripped away by the memory of her lifeless body on the forest floor.

I failed her.

The thought stabs through me like a dagger, twisting deeper with every passing second. I should've done something, should've been strong enough to protect her. But instead,

I stood there, powerless and useless.

"Asterine," Neville's voice pulls me from my spiraling thoughts. He's seated across the room, his face pale and drawn. "You okay?"

I nod, though the gesture feels hollow. "Yeah. Just… thinking."

Before he can respond, the heavy wooden doors burst open with a loud bang.

Headmaster Dimick storms into the room, his normally composed demeanor replaced by a palpable tension. His dark robes billow around him as he strides forward, his sharp eyes scanning each of us in turn.

"What happened?" he demands, his voice ringing with a mix of fear and frustration.

None of us answer at first, the weight of his question hanging in the air. Finally, my mother steps forward, her expression calm but weary. "We need to talk."

Dimick's gaze snaps to her, his eyes narrowing. "Talk? About what? You disappear for days, return with bloodied children, and you expect me to wait patiently for an explanation?"

"It's not that simple," my father interjects, his tone firm.

"Then make it simple," Dimick snaps. "Because right now, I'm looking at a group of students who have clearly been through hell, and I have no idea why."

The silence in the room is suffocating, heavy with tension and unspoken truths. The faint morning light filters through the stained-glass windows, casting fragmented patterns across the stone floor. It's almost too serene, too normal, for what we've just endured.

Maeve is gone.

That thought alone should be enough to shatter me, to send

me spiraling into the depths of despair. And yet, it's not just Maeve's death weighing on me. It's everything—the lies, the secrets, the betrayals.

"Someone needs to start talking," Headmaster Dimick snaps, his usually calm demeanor replaced by sharp-edged urgency. He stands in the middle of the room, his dark robes billowing as he turns to face my parents. "What in the name of sanity happened out there?"

My father exchanges a glance with my mother, their expressions tight with exhaustion and unease. For a moment, no one speaks, the silence stretching thin like a taut string ready to snap.

"It was Valora," my mother finally says, her voice steady but soft. "The Vampire Queen. She attacked us."

Dimick's face darkens, his sharp features tightening. "Valora? She's supposed to be in exile. How did she—"

"She's not in exile," my father interrupts, his tone grim. "She's been building an army, waiting for the right moment to strike. And we walked right into her trap."

My mother takes a deep breath, stepping forward. "We were ambushed in the forest. Valora's guards, her reinforcements... they came out of nowhere. She wanted Asterine."

Dimick's gaze shifts to me, his eyes narrowing. "And why is that?"

I shrink under his scrutiny, my chest tightening as the weight of his words settles over me.

"Because of what she is," my father says quietly. "Because of her powers."

Dimick pinches the bridge of his nose, letting out a heavy sigh. "So she knows."

"Yes," my mother confirms, her voice trembling slightly.

"She's known for years. She sent Evander to manipulate Asterine, to lure her into her grasp. And when that failed, she sent her guards."

The mention of Evander sends a shiver down my spine. His face flashes in my mind—his piercing eyes, his charming smile, the way he made me feel like I was the center of his world. And then the betrayal, the cold realization that it was all a lie.

I clench my fists, my nails biting into my palms as I try to push the memories away.

Dimick paces the room, his movements sharp and agitated. "So let me get this straight," he says, his voice laced with frustration. "You knew Valora was a threat. You knew she was targeting Asterine. And yet, you kept her in the dark?"

"She was safer not knowing," my mother says, her tone defensive.

"Was she?" Dimick counters, his voice rising. "Because from where I'm standing, keeping her in the dark nearly got all of you killed!"

"We were trying to protect her!" my father snaps, his calm facade cracking.

"Protect her?" I cut in, my voice trembling with anger. "By lying to me? By hiding everything from me while the rest of you played your secret games?"

"Asterine, it wasn't like that," Neville says, stepping forward.

"Then what was it like, Neville?" I demand, my voice sharp. "Because from where I'm standing, it feels a hell of a lot like betrayal."

My mother turns to me, her eyes soft but pleading. "We didn't tell you because we didn't want you to carry this burden. You were just a child, Asterine. We thought if we could keep you safe, if we could shield you from all of this, you could have a normal life."

"A normal life?" I laugh bitterly, the sound harsh and hollow. "Do you honestly think I've had a normal life? Do you think hiding my powers, pretending to be something I'm not, felt normal?"

"We made mistakes," my father admits, his voice heavy with regret. "We thought we were doing what was best for you, but… maybe we were wrong."

"Maybe?" I snap, my voice rising.

Neville steps closer, his expression earnest. "Asterine, I know you're angry, and you have every right to be. But you need to understand—this wasn't just about keeping you safe. It was about keeping everyone safe. If Valora had gotten to you earlier…"

He trails off, his words hanging in the air like a heavy weight.

His words cut deep, the truth of them undeniable. I know he's right. I know they all are. But that doesn't make it hurt any less.

They lied to me. They kept me in the dark, made decisions about my life without ever giving me a say. And now, because of their choices, Maeve is dead, Fabian is broken, and I… I don't even know who I am anymore.

My chest tightens, a sharp ache spreading through my ribs. I want to scream, to cry, to lash out, but all I can do is stand there, the weight of their words pressing down on me.

Dimick clears his throat, drawing the room's attention back to him. "If Valora knows about Asterine's powers, then she's not going to stop. This wasn't a one-off attack. She'll come back, and next time, she'll bring everything she has."

My stomach twists, fear curling in my chest like a living thing.

"So what do we do?" Ryker asks, his midnight-black eyes fixed on Dimick.

Dimick's gaze shifts to my parents, his expression grim. "We tell her everything. No more secrets, no more lies. She needs to know the full truth."

My mother stiffens, her face paling. "It's not the right time—"

"There is no right time," Dimick cuts her off. "Not anymore. If you keep waiting for the perfect moment, you'll never tell her. And she'll never be ready for what's coming."

"What truth?" I ask, my voice trembling.

No one answers, their silence more telling than any words could be.

# 39

# A New Path

The tension in the room is palpable, thick enough to choke on. Dimick paces back and forth, his dark robes swishing around his ankles as he rubs his temples, clearly grappling with whatever he's about to say.

Everyone is on edge, their expressions ranging from confusion to exhaustion. My parents sit stiffly on the worn leather sofa, their hands clasped tightly together. Neville stands by the window, his gaze fixed on the moonlit courtyard outside. Ryker leans against the door frame, his midnight-black eyes sharp and unreadable.

And me? I'm trying not to explode.

The weight of their revelations still presses down on me, heavy and unrelenting. I feel like a balloon stretched to its limit, ready to burst at the slightest nudge.

Finally, Dimick stops pacing and turns to face us, his expression grim. "There's only one way to fix this."

"Fix what, exactly?" I ask, my voice sharper than I intended.

He doesn't flinch, meeting my gaze head-on. "Your future. Your place in this world. And the threat Valora poses to all of us."

Dimick crosses his arms, his tone steady and deliberate. "Asterine, you need to finish your high school education sooner. It's time to step away from the mundane and embrace what you are. What you were born to be."

The words hit me like a punch to the gut. "You want me to... what? Drop out and do what, exactly?"

"You don't have to drop out," he clarifies, his voice calm but firm. "You accelerate. Finish your courses early, take your exams, and graduate. Then, you focus on Paranormal Arts—combat, magic, diplomacy. The skills you'll need to survive and lead."

"Lead?" My voice trembles, the enormity of the word crashing down on me.

Dimick nods, his expression softening slightly. "You have the potential to be something this world hasn't seen in centuries, Asterine. A unifier. A Queen."

A stunned silence falls over the room. My heart pounds in my chest, each beat louder than the last.

"A Queen?" Neville finally breaks the silence, his voice laced with disbelief.

"Yes," Dimick says simply.

Dimick turns to me, his gaze steady. "You have the strength and power to unite the supernatural factions. The vampires, the werewolves, the witches, and every other being that walks this earth. But they won't accept you just because you exist. You'll have to prove yourself to them."

"How?" I manage to ask, my voice barely above a whisper.

He hesitates for a moment before continuing. "You'll call a meeting. A Conclave of Kings and Queens. All the leaders of the supernatural factions in one place. And you'll challenge them."

The air leaves the room, everyone's eyes snapping to Dimick in disbelief.

"Challenge them?" Ryker's voice is sharp, his midnight-black eyes narrowing. "To what, exactly?"

"To a fight," Dimick says, his tone matter-of-fact. "They'll test you. Each faction will put forth their strongest to face you in combat. If you can defeat them, they'll have no choice but to acknowledge your strength and your right to lead."

"No," my mother says instantly, her voice trembling with anger. She rises to her feet, her hands shaking. "Absolutely not."

My father stands as well, his expression equally stormy. "This is madness. She's a child, Dimick. You're asking her to go up against beings who have centuries of experience. Do you know what you're asking of her?"

"I do," Dimick replies evenly. "And I wouldn't suggest it if I didn't believe she could do it."

"She's not ready," my mother snaps. "She's barely had time to process what she is, let alone fight supernatural royalty!"

"She's more ready than you think," Dimick counters. "She defeated Valora's guards. She siphoned Valora herself. That kind of power doesn't need years of preparation. It needs focus. Training. Purpose."

I can feel their words swirling around me, their arguments blurring into a cacophony of voices. My chest tightens, my breathing quickening as I try to process everything.

"Stop," I say quietly, my voice trembling.

No one hears me.

"Stop," I say again, louder this time.

The room goes silent, all eyes turning to me.

"I'm not a child," I say, my voice steady despite the storm raging inside me. "And I'm done letting all of you decide what's best for me. I'll do it."

"Asterine, no," Neville says, stepping forward. "You don't have to do this."

"Yes, I do," I reply, meeting his gaze. "You said it yourself, Neville. This isn't just about me. It's about everyone. If I can stop Valora, if I can unite the factions, then maybe all of this—Maeve, the guards, everything—won't be for nothing."

"You're not thinking clearly," my mother says, her voice pleading. "You're angry, you're hurt—"

"Of course I'm angry!" I shout, my voice cracking. "I'm angry because all of you have been lying to me my entire life! I'm angry because I had to find out who I am the hard way, in the middle of a battlefield! And I'm angry because Maeve is dead, and I couldn't do anything to stop it!"

Tears blur my vision, but I blink them away, refusing to let them fall. "But this… this is something I can do. This is something I have to do."

Dimick steps forward, his expression softening. "You're right, Asterine. This is your choice. And if you choose to do this, I'll help you. We all will."

"Dimick," my mother begins, her voice trembling.

"She's not a child anymore," Dimick says gently. "She's the most powerful siphoner born in centuries. You can't protect her forever. It's time to let her be who she's meant to be."

His words hit me like a lightning strike, sharp and electrifying. Who I'm meant to be.

The truth is, I don't know who that is. I don't know if I'm ready to be a leader, to face the supernatural factions and fight for my place. But I do know one thing: I'm tired of being afraid.

I'm tired of hiding.

For so long, I've felt like a passenger in my own life, swept along by the decisions of others. But now… now I have a chance to take control. To be more than just a girl with powers she doesn't understand.

I glance around the room, taking in the faces of the people I love. My parents, their worry etched into every line of their faces. Neville, his jaw tight with frustration. Ryker, his midnight-black eyes watching me with an intensity that makes my heart race.

This is my family. My friends. And I'll do whatever it takes to protect them.

"I'll do it," I say again, my voice firm.

Dimick nods, his expression resolute. "Then it's time to start preparing. We'll call the Conclave, and you'll face the leaders of every faction."

My mother shakes her head, tears streaming down her face. "Asterine, please—"

"No," I say firmly, cutting her off. "This is my decision. And I'm not backing down."

The room falls silent, the weight of my words settling over everyone like a heavy blanket. I can feel the tension, the fear, the uncertainty radiating from them, but I refuse to let it shake me.

For the first time in my life, I feel like I'm in control.

# 40

# Farewell

The sound of the shower fills the small bathroom, water pelting against the tile in a relentless rhythm. I stand under the stream, my head bowed, my arms wrapped around myself as if I can hold everything in. The heat fogs up the mirror, turning the room into a hazy cocoon, but it doesn't ease the tightness in my chest.

Maeve is gone.

The thought circles back like a broken record, each repetition cutting deeper than the last. I close my eyes, the water cascading over my face, and try to focus on the sensation. It doesn't help.

It should've been me.

I clench my fists, my nails digging into my palms. If I had been stronger, faster, more aware… maybe Maeve would still be alive. Maybe Fabian wouldn't have to carry her broken body through the portal, his face etched with a grief so profound it was unbearable to witness.

The tears come, mixing with the water streaming down my face. I don't bother wiping them away. No one can see me here, hidden behind the steam and the sound of the water.

I think about Maeve's smile, her sharp wit, the way she always managed to lighten the mood no matter how dire the situation. And now, because of me, she's gone.

This is my fault. All of it.

I should've been more prepared. I should've understood my powers sooner, learned how to control them. Instead, I spent years pretending to be normal, hiding from the truth of what I am.

A knock on the bathroom door pulls me from my spiraling thoughts.

"Asterine, are you okay in there?" Eira's voice is soft but tinged with concern.

"I'm fine," I manage to say, though my voice cracks slightly.

"You've been in there for a while," she continues. "I just… wanted to check."

"I'll be out in a minute," I reply, forcing my tone to steady.

There's a pause, and then I hear her footsteps retreating.

I take a deep breath, trying to ground myself. The funeral is today. Maeve's parents are coming. I can't fall apart. Not yet.

When I finally step out of the shower, the cold air hits me like a slap, and I shiver despite the heat lingering on my skin. I wrap a towel around myself and move to the mirror, wiping away the fog with a trembling hand.

My reflection stares back at me, pale and drawn, dark circles under my eyes from too many sleepless nights. I barely recognize the girl in the mirror.

I dress quickly, pulling on a simple black dress and brushing my hair into some semblance of order. The dress feels heavy, constricting, like it's absorbing the weight of everything I'm carrying.

When I step into the dorm room, Eira is sitting on her bed, her hands folded in her lap. She looks up as I enter, her expression soft but serious.

"You look…" Eira trails off, searching for the right word.

"Like a mess?" I offer, forcing a small, humorless smile.

She shakes her head. "Like you're carrying the weight of the world."

I sit down on my bed, the mattress creaking slightly under my weight. "It feels that way."

Eira shifts, turning to face me fully. "You don't have to do this alone, you know. We're all here for you."

I nod, though the gesture feels hollow. "I know. It's just… Maeve's parents are coming. And they're going to hate me."

"They won't hate you," Eira says quickly, but there's a flicker of doubt in her eyes.

"They should," I reply, my voice trembling. "Maeve's dead because of me. Because I wasn't strong enough to protect her."

Eira leans forward, her gaze steady. "Maeve wouldn't want you to blame yourself, Asterine. She knew the risks, just like all of us. This isn't your fault."

"It feels like it is," I whisper.

Eira reaches out, her hand resting on mine. "You're not alone in this, okay? Whatever happens today, we'll face it together."

The sky is overcast as we step outside, the heavy clouds casting a dull, gray light over the academy grounds. A light drizzle begins to fall, the rain cool against my skin as we make our way to the courtyard where the funeral is being held.

The atmosphere is somber, the air thick with unspoken grief. Fabian stands by the makeshift altar, his face unreadable as he gazes down at Maeve's wrapped body. Jocosa is beside him, her hands glowing faintly as she whispers a quiet prayer.

My parents are here too, standing off to the side with Neville. Their expressions are grim, their gazes heavy as they watch the proceedings.

And then I see them.

Maeve's parents.

They're tall, imposing figures with the same sharp features and piercing eyes that Maeve had. Her father's jaw is clenched, his fists tight at his sides, while her mother's expression is one of barely contained fury.

When their eyes land on me, it's like a physical blow.

"You," Maeve's mother hisses, her voice low and venomous.

I freeze, my heart pounding in my chest.

"You were supposed to protect her," she continues, her tone rising. "You were supposed to keep her safe!"

"I—I tried," I stammer, my voice barely above a whisper.

"Tried?" her father snaps, his voice like thunder. "She's dead because of you! If you hadn't dragged her into this—"

"That's enough," Neville cuts in, stepping between us. His voice is calm but firm, his gaze steady as he faces them. "This isn't the time or place."

Maeve's father glares at him, his fists trembling. "You think I care about time or place? My daughter is gone!"

"And blaming Asterine won't bring her back," Neville replies, his tone unyielding.

Maeve's mother steps forward, her eyes blazing. "You have no idea what we've lost. If we ever see you again, girl," she says, turning her gaze to me, "you'll get a taste of your own medicine."

Her words hang in the air like a curse, sharp and unrelenting.

The funeral proceeds in heavy silence. Fabian places Maeve's body into the ground, his hands trembling as he shovels the first mound of dirt over her. Jocosa murmurs another prayer, her voice soft and trembling.

I stand at the edge of the group, my hands clenched into fists at my sides. The rain has picked up, the droplets mixing with the tears streaming down my face.

When it's over, the crowd begins to disperse, leaving behind the freshly turned earth and a hollow ache in my chest.

As I walk back to the dorm, Eira falls into step beside me. Neither of us speaks, the weight of the day pressing down on us like a tangible force.

But as we reach the door, a thought takes root in my mind.

This isn't over.

Maeve's parents may hate me, the others may blame me, but I won't let her death be in vain.

I'll make sure of it.

# Epilogue

The moonlight filters through the towering Gothic spires of Harlow Academy, casting long, silver shadows across the courtyard. The air is crisp and cool, carrying with it the faint scent of damp earth from the earlier rain. I stand near the edge of the garden, my arms wrapped around myself as I try to find the courage to move.

I've been standing here for what feels like hours, staring up at the window of Ryker's dorm.

What am I even going to say?

The past few days have been a whirlwind of revelations and losses, each one more crushing than the last. But amidst it all, one thought has refused to leave my mind: Ryker.

He lost his mother—not in the way I lost the parents I thought I knew, but in a much crueler, sharper way. The Queen had abandoned him, betrayed him, and used him.

And yet, when I was in danger, when Vance dragged me through that portal, it was Ryker who came for me. Ryker, who put himself at risk without hesitation.

I need to see him.

Taking a deep breath, I force my legs to move, stepping toward the building. The heavy wooden door creaks slightly as I push it open, the sound echoing in the quiet hallway. The faint glow of candlelight spills from under Ryker's door, a beacon guiding me forward.

I knock softly, my heart pounding in my chest.

"Come in," his voice calls, low and steady.

I push the door open and step inside.

Ryker is sitting by the window, his copper hair tousled, his midnight-black eyes reflecting the moonlight. He looks up as I enter, his expression softening when he sees me.

"Asterine," he says quietly, his voice tinged with surprise. "What are you doing here?"

I close the door behind me, my fingers trembling slightly. "I wanted to check on you. After everything that's happened… I just—I needed to see you."

His lips curve into a faint smile, though it doesn't reach his eyes. "You're the one who's been through hell, and yet, you're worried about me."

I move to sit across from him, my hands clasped tightly in my lap. "I know what you've been through, Ryker. And I can't stop thinking about it. About everything."

He leans back in his chair, his gaze fixed on me. "Everything," he repeats, his voice heavy. "Where do we even start?"

"The library," I say softly, my heart twisting at the memory. "When you came to save me… Ryker, I can't stop thinking about what would've happened if you hadn't shown up."

His jaw tightens, his midnight eyes darkening. "And I can't stop thinking about the fact that I couldn't stop Vance from taking you. I was right there, Asterine. I should've—"

"You did everything you could," I interrupt, my voice firm. "You came for me when no one else could. You saved me, Ryker."

He shakes his head, his hands balling into fists. "But I didn't stop it from happening. I didn't stop Vance, and I didn't stop my mother."

The mention of the Queen sends a chill through me. "Ryker," I say gently, "none of this is your fault. She's… she's your mother. I can't imagine what that must feel like."

His eyes glisten, the pain in them raw and unguarded. "She's not my mother," he says bitterly. "A mother doesn't abandon her child. A mother doesn't use her child like a pawn in some twisted game. She made her choice, Asterine. And it wasn't me."

I reach out, my hand brushing against his. "Ryker…"

He looks down at our hands, his expression softening. "And yet, even after everything she's done, I still can't help but wonder what I did wrong. Why I wasn't enough."

My heart aches at his words, the vulnerability in them cutting deeper than any blade. "You didn't do anything wrong," I say, my voice trembling. "You're enough, Ryker. More than enough."

The silence stretches between us, heavy with unspoken words.

"And Maeve," he says finally, his voice breaking. "She shouldn't have died, Asterine. None of this should've happened."

I nod, my throat tightening. "I keep thinking about her, too. About what I could've done differently."

"She was brave," he says, his midnight-black eyes locking onto mine. "She fought until the very end. But her death… it wasn't your fault, Asterine. You need to stop blaming yourself."

"I don't know how," I admit, my voice barely above a whisper.

"You start by realizing that you're not alone," he says, his voice steady. "You have us. You have me."

I look down at our intertwined hands, the warmth of his touch grounding me. "And now I'm supposed to fight the leaders of every supernatural faction," I say, my voice laced with disbelief. "Dimick thinks I can unite them, but I don't even know if I can keep myself together."

Ryker's lips curve into a faint smile. "If anyone can do it, it's you."

I shake my head, the weight of his faith in me both comforting and terrifying. "I'm scared, Ryker. What if I fail? What if I can't do this?"

"Then you'll try again," he says simply. "And again, until you succeed. Because that's who you are, Asterine. You don't give up. You fight."

His words stir something inside me, a flicker of hope in the midst of the chaos.

"And whatever happens," he continues, his voice soft but firm, "I'm not going anywhere. I'll be right there with you, every step of the way."

I look up at him, my heart pounding. "You will?"

"Always," he says, his midnight-black eyes shining with determination. "I'll graduate faster, just like you. We'll face the factions together. Whatever comes next, we'll do it together."

The emotion in his voice is overwhelming, and I feel my own tears start to fall. "Ryker..."

Ryker's midnight eyes meet mine, and for a moment, the tension between us is palpable. His walls are up, but there's a crack—a flicker of vulnerability he can't hide. "I've lost too much already," he says, his voice barely audible. The unspoken words hang between us, heavy with meaning: "Don't let me lose you too."

He leans closer, his hand cupping my cheek. "Asterine, I... I like you. More than I ever thought I could like anyone."

My breath catches, my heart pounding in my chest. "I like

you too," I whisper, the words feeling both terrifying and exhilarating.

He smiles, his thumb brushing away a tear. "Then we're in this together."

I nod, a faint smile breaking through my tears. "Together."

He pulls me into an embrace, his arms wrapping around me like a shield against the chaos of the world. For the first time in days, I feel safe.

As we sit there, holding each other in the dim light of his dorm, I realize something.

No matter what comes next—no matter the challenges, the battles, the betrayals—I'm not alone.

And for now, that's enough.

# Acknowledgments

*"Cold Games Part 2: The Game of Secrets"* has been a labor of love, and it wouldn't have been possible without the support of so many wonderful people.

First and foremost, I want to thank my family and friends for their immense belief in me, even on the days when I doubted myself. Your encouragement gave me the strength to keep writing.

To my readers, both old and new, thank you for venturing on this journey with me. Your enthusiasm for the world of *Cold Games* fuels my creativity and keeps me striving to bring these characters to life.

A heartfelt thanks to those who offered feedback and shared their thoughts. Your input and support have been invaluable in shaping this story.

Lastly, to anyone who has ever dreamt of creating their own world through words: keep going. Your stories matter, and your voice deserves to be heard.

Thank you all for being part of this adventure.

With gratitude,

**Amiti**

AMITI
COLD GAMES
PART II:
THE GAME OF SECRETS
CHALLENGES MAKE YOU STRONGER, BUT HOW CAN IT
JUSTIFY LOSING SOMEONE YOU LOVE?

To be continued…
    Cold Games Part III: The Game of Realms